THE DEATH OF IVAN ILYICH

AND

MASTER AND MAN

LEO TOLSTOY

THE DEATH OF
IVAN ILYICH
AND
MASTER AND MAN

A new translation, with an Introduction and Notes,

by Ann Pasternak Slater

THE MODERN LIBRARY

NEW YORK

LIBRARY OF CONGRESS CATALOGING-IN-PUBLICATION DATA
Tolstoy, Leo, graf, 1828–1910.
[Smert' Ivana Il'icha. English]
The death of Ivan Ilyich; and, Master and man / Leo Tolstoy; a new
translation, with an introduction and notes, by Ann Pasternak Slater.
p.   cm.
ISBN 0-375-76099-7
I. Pasternak Slater, Ann. II. Tolstoy, Leo, graf, 1828–1910.
Khoziain i rabotnik. English. III. Title: Master and man. IV. Title.
PG3366.S6   2003
891.73'3—dc21 2003051046

8   9   7

LEO TOLSTOY

Count Lev (Leo) Nikolayevich Tolstoy was born on August 28, 1828, at Yasnaya Polyana (Bright Glade), his family's estate located 130 miles southwest of Moscow. He was the fourth of five children born to Count Nikolay Ilyich Tolstoy and Marya Nikolayevna Tolstoya (née Princess Volkonskaya, who died when Tolstoy was barely two). He enjoyed a privileged childhood typical of his elevated social class (his patrician family was older and prouder than the tsar's). Early on, the boy showed a gift for languages as well as a fondness for literature—including fairy tales, the poems of Pushkin, and the Bible, especially the Old Testament story of Joseph. Orphaned at the age of nine by the death of his father, Tolstoy and his brothers and sister were first cared for by a devoutly religious aunt. When she died in 1841 the family went to live with their father's only surviving sister in the provincial city of Kazan. Tolstoy was educated by French and German tutors until he enrolled at Kazan University in 1844. There he studied law and Oriental languages and developed a keen interest in moral philosophy and the writings of Rousseau. A notably unsuccessful student who led a dissolute life, Tolstoy abandoned his studies in 1847 without earning a degree and returned to Yasnaya Polyana to claim the property (along with 350 serfs and their families) that was his birthright.

After several aimless years of debauchery and gambling in Moscow and St. Petersburg, Tolstoy journeyed to the Caucasus in 1851 to join his older brother Nikolay, an army lieutenant participating in the Caucasian campaign. The following year Tolstoy officially enlisted in the military, and in 1854 he became a commissioned officer in the artillery, serving first on the Danube and later in the Crimean War. Although his sexual escapades and profligate gambling during this period shocked even his fellow soldiers, it was while in the army that Tolstoy began his literary apprenticeship. Greatly influenced by the works of Charles Dickens, Tolstoy wrote *Childhood*, his first novel. Published pseudonymously in September 1852 in the *Contemporary*, a St. Petersburg journal, the book received highly favorable reviews—earning the praise of Turgenev—and overnight established Tolstoy as a major writer. Over the next years he contributed several novels and short stories (about military life) to the *Contemporary*—including *Boyhood* (1854), three Sevastopol stories (1855–1856), "Two Hussars" (1856), and *Youth* (1857).

In 1856 Tolstoy left the army and went to live in St. Petersburg, where he was much in demand in fashionable salons. He quickly discovered, however, that he disliked the life of a literary celebrity (he often quarreled with fellow writers, especially Turgenev) and soon departed on his first trip to western Europe. Upon returning to Russia, he produced the story "Three Deaths" and a short novel, *Family Happiness*, both published in 1859. Afterward, Tolstoy decided to abandon literature in favor of more "useful" pursuits. He retired to Yasnaya Polyana to manage his estate and established a school there for the education of children of his serfs. In 1860 he again traveled abroad in order to observe European (especially German) educational systems; he later published *Yasnaya Polyana*, a journal expounding his theories on pedagogy. The following year he was appointed an arbiter of the peace to settle disputes between newly emancipated serfs and their former masters. But in July 1862 the police raided the school at Yasnaya Polyana for evidence of subversive activity. The search elicited an indignant protest from Tolstoy directly to Alexander II, who officially exonerated him.

That same summer, at the age of thirty-four, Tolstoy fell in love with eighteen-year-old Sofya Andreyevna Bers, who was living with her parents on a nearby estate. (As a girl she had reverently memorized whole passages of *Childhood*.) The two were married on September 23, 1862, in a church inside the Kremlin walls. The early years of the marriage were largely joyful (thirteen children were born of the union) and coincided with the period of Tolstoy's great novels. In 1863 he not only published *The Cossacks*, but began work on *War and Peace*, his great epic novel that came out in 1869.

Then, on March 18, 1873, inspired by the opening of a fragmentary tale by Pushkin, Tolstoy started writing *Anna Karenina*. Originally titled *Two Marriages*, the book underwent multiple revisions and was serialized to great popular and critical acclaim between 1875 and 1877.

It was during the torment of writing *Anna Karenina* that Tolstoy experienced the spiritual crisis that recast the rest of his life. Haunted by the inevitability of death, he underwent a "conversion" to the ideals of human life and conduct that he found in the teachings of Christ. *A Confession* (1882), which was banned in Russia, marked this change in his life and works. Afterward, he became an extreme rationalist and moralist, and in a series of pamphlets published during his remaining years Tolstoy rejected both church and state, denounced private ownership of property, and advocated celibacy, even in marriage. In 1897 he even went so far as to denounce his own novels, as well as many other classics, including Shakespeare's *King Lear* and Beethoven's Ninth Symphony, for being morally irresponsible, elitist, and corrupting. His teachings earned him numerous followers in Russia ("We have two tsars, Nicholas II and Leo Tolstoy," a journalist wrote) and abroad (most notably, Mahatma Gandhi) but also many opponents, and in 1901 he was excommunicated by the Russian holy synod. Prompted by Turgenev's deathbed entreaty ("My friend, return to literature!"), Tolstoy did produce several more short stories and novels—including the ongoing series *Stories for the People*, "The Death of Ivan Ilyich" (1886), *The Kreutzer Sonata* (1889), "Master and Man" (1895), *Resurrection* (1899), and *Hadji Murat* (published posthumously)—as well as a play, *The Power of Darkness* (1886).

Tolstoy's controversial views produced a great strain on his marriage, and his relationship with his wife deteriorated. "Until the day I die she will be a stone around my neck," he wrote. "I must learn not to drown with this stone around my neck." Finally, on the morning of October 28,

1910, Tolstoy fled by railroad from Yasnaya Polyana headed for a monastery in search of peace and solitude. However, illness forced Tolstoy off the train at Astapovo; he was given refuge in the stationmaster's house and died there on November 7. His body was buried two days later in the forest at Yasnaya Polyana.

CONTENTS

INTRODUCTION

Ann Pasternak Slater

1

"The Death of Ivan Ilyich" and "Master and Man" are Tolstoy's late masterpieces. Written well after *War and Peace* and *Anna Karenina*, both stories directly confront the long, uneventful process of dying, some two decades before Tolstoy's own death at the railway station of Astapovo. Yet both stories also draw on experiences described in his earliest work and resolve some of the questions overwhelming him during his crisis of faith in the 1880s.

The story begins in late January 1854. Tolstoy was twenty-five years old and on his way home from fighting in the Caucasus. It was the worst of the winter. There were no trains. Tolstoy's diary is laconic:

> On the road. Was lost all night at Belogorodtsevskaya, 100 versts from Cherkassk, and the idea occurred to me of writing a story, "The Snowstorm." ... Nothing on the road cheered me so much and so reminded me of Russia as a baggage horse which laid back its ears and despite the speed of my sledge tried to overtake it at a gallop.

"The Snowstorm" was written two years later. It is a scrupulously flat account of a night's sleigh ride across a featureless steppe through an intense blizzard. The narrator distrusts his surly driver who, he suspects, is a novice. They set out at dusk, and soon lose their way. They halt repeatedly. The coachman climbs down and plunges about in the snow trying to find the road. They decide to turn back. Bells jingling tunefully, three troikas carrying the mail drive past. They turn again, follow the troikas, and lose them. They get lost once more. This time, the narrator dismounts and casts about in the snow. In the force field of the blizzard, he loses his bearings.

A moment's anxiety before he touches the invisible sleigh right next to him.

Once again they decide to turn back—and meet the troikas returning. They follow them. En route, they overtake a long, slow wagon train. Then they lose the road. For a long time they have no sense of direction. They seem to be going in circles—and here is the baggage train they had left behind them, a dark line on the horizon ahead, still moving steadily onward.

It is bitterly cold. His fellow passengers fret about death from exposure, but the narrator insists on continuing their blind journey. He dozes off and remembers with incomparable vividness a hot day on the estate, when a young peasant drowned in the pond. . . .

Many details of this patiently monotonous story contribute to "Master and Man," another journey through a snowstorm, written forty years later. But the two stories have a radically different atmosphere. In "The Snowstorm," the characters reach their destination safely as the sun rises. There is a much larger cast of travelers. In company, danger seems more remote, whereas in "Master and Man" there is a strong sense of headstrong, vulnerable isolation. In "The Snowstorm," death is a hypothesis repeatedly canvassed—and ignored. The actuality of death is raised only obliquely in the episode of the drowned peasant. This casualness seems characteristic not only of the youthful narrator but of Tolstoy himself. When he completed the story in February 1856, he wrote in his diary: "Quarreled with Turgenev, and had a girl at my place. . . . Finished 'The Snowstorm.' I'm very pleased with it." There is an apparent thoughtlessness here that would be unthinkable for the later Tolstoy.

And yet the diary entry is disingenuous. In 1856, his elder brother Dmitri lay dying of tuberculosis. "I'm terribly depressed," Tolstoy noted baldly. "From tomorrow I want to spend my days in such a way that it will be pleasant to recall them. I'll put my papers in order...do a fair copy of 'The Snowstorm.'...." Later, Tolstoy wrote in his *Reminiscences:* Dmitri "did not want to die, did not want to believe he was about to die." Did Dmitri's deliberate denial, his blind refusal, become "The Snowstorm's" insouciance in the face of death? Is that insouciance therefore ironic—carrying its own charge of covert criticism? Should we rather look death directly in the face?

———

A year later, in Paris in March 1857, the tourist Tolstoy took in the sights and touched on the same bruised spot:

> Got up at 7 feeling ill and went to see an execution. A stout, white, strong neck and chest. He kissed the Gospels and then— death. How senseless! The impression it made was a strong one and not wasted on me. Morality and art. I know, I love, and I can.

The last line of that diary entry is significant, and will reverberate through Tolstoy's later work.

One immediate consequence was a slight story, "Three Deaths," written in January 1858. It contrasts the deaths of a lady, a peasant, and a tree. Predictably, the lady anticipates death with terrified evasion. She is traveling to Italy in vain hope of a cure, her entourage of bullied lady's maid, doctor, and weak husband reluctantly in tow. The stuffy carriage smells of eau de cologne and dust. Terminally tubercular, fretful, and self-deceiving, the lady is, as Tolstoy wrote to a friend, "pitiful and bad." Every failure to help her face death is sentimentally justified: "Oh my God!" her husband says. "Think of me, having to remind her about her will. I can't tell her that."

At a coaching inn where they stop for refreshments, a dying peasant coughs on the Dutch oven in the kitchen. Sergei, the coachman's boy, asks him a favor: "I expect you don't need your new boots now; won't you let me have them?" "Need them indeed!" the cook snaps. "What does he want with boots? They won't bury him in boots." The euphemistic lies of the gentry contrast sharply with brutal peasant honesty. In mild acquiescence, the dying man gives up his unused new boots. The coachman's boy agrees to put a stone on his grave in exchange.

That night the peasant dies in his sleep. Next spring, the lady dies in her town house, without ever reaching Italy. Even as she receives the last sacrament her attention is distracted by the priest's recommendation of a local quack. Later, the deacon reads the Psalms over the dead body—monotonously, through his nose, without understanding the words. But beyond the door of the death chamber, there is renewal—children's voices and the patter of feet. And what do the words of the Psalms actually say? They, too, speak of renewal. "Thou hidest thy face, they are troubled: thou takest away their breath, they die, and return to their dust. Thou sendest forth thy spirit, they are created: and thou renewest the face of the earth."

In the coaching inn, the cook rebukes Sergei, the coachman's boy, for failing to keep his promise. If he can't afford a stone, he should at least mark the grave with a wooden cross.

As the dawn mists disperse, Sergei's axe strokes can be heard, and a tree falls.

Tolstoy's letter about this parable is explicit. The lady has lied all her life and lies in the face of death. Her understanding of Christianity cannot resolve the questions of life and death. The peasant dies in peaceful accord with the natural laws that governed his years of sowing and harvesting, delivering calves and slaughtering cattle. The tree dies "calmly, honestly, and gracefully." The adverbs are pointedly anthropomorphic.

The loaded contrast between the gentry's reluctance to confront death and the equanimity of the peasants, who have known a lifetime's hardship, recurs in "The Death of Ivan Ilyich" and "Master and Man." The irrelevance of formal religion is also repeated, and its rituals are satirized. And, like the lady of this story, as Ivan Ilyich receives the last sacrament, he is momentarily tempted by the promise of a curative operation.

A decade after writing "Three Deaths," in August 1869, soon after fin-ishing *War and Peace,* Tolstoy heard of land for sale in the distant Penza province. As he wrote later, "I wanted to buy an estate so that the income from it, or the timber on it, should cover the whole purchase price and I should get it for nothing. I looked out for some fool who did not under-stand business, and thought that I had found such a man." In high good humor, he set out with one servant and decided to cover the long last lap of the journey without stopping. Dozing through the night, he woke with a sudden sense of horror and futility:

> "Why am I going? Where am I going to?" I suddenly asked myself. It was not that I did not like the idea of buying an estate cheaply, but it suddenly oc-curred to me that there was no need for me to travel all that distance, that I should die here in this strange place, and I was filled with dread.

So they stopped at a small post station, woke up the attendant, and were shown into the only bedroom. The place was called Arzamas.

In his biography of Tolstoy, Henri Troyat makes the experience a melodrama in the style of Poe. The room was white and square, "like a big coffin." The furniture was soiled. "The doors and woodwork [were] painted dark red, a color of dried blood." Shaken by his sudden horror of death, "questions fell upon him like a flock of ravens. . . . He was the only person awake on a sinking ship."

Tolstoy's own account is drier. It is normality that frightens him. "A sleepy man with a spot on his cheek (which seemed to me terrifying) showed us into a small square room with whitewashed walls. I remember it tormented me that it should be square. It had one window with a red curtain." He fell asleep, only to awake in renewed terror. Death was in the room with him. *It* followed him into the corridor in search of his sleeping servant. Everything seemed to be saying the same thing: "There is nothing in life. Death is the only real thing, and death ought not to exist." In what we would now identify as a panic attack, it seems Tolstoy felt he was dying.

Life and death somehow merged into one another. Something was tearing my soul apart and could not complete the severance.... Again I went to look at the sleepers, and again I tried to go to sleep. Always the same horror: red, white and square. Something tearing within that yet could not be torn apart. A painful, painfully dry and spiteful feeling, no atom of kindliness....

Like the Ancient Mariner, Tolstoy tried to pray, surreptitiously glancing over his shoulder in case anyone was watching him. In vain. No prayers would come. He woke his servant and they left in the dark. When they reached their destination, Tolstoy did not buy the land. He was forty-one years old.

———

Another decade passed. As letters to his wife, Sofya, and the reminiscences of his son Sergei testify, Tolstoy continued to experience terrifying intimations of death. When *Anna Karenina* was finished in 1877, he began *A Confession,* a self-critical, clear-sighted, autobiographical account of his deepening spiritual crisis. In form, its first half is comparable to the narrative of "The Death of Ivan Ilyich." Decades are sweepingly surveyed, significant moments seized on and coldly scrutinized. The content, too, is similar. Tolstoy categorically condemns his decade of early maturity from about 1845 to 1855, when he indulged his machismo—womanizing, quarreling, even killing in his army years. At that time, he had believed in a popular concept of "progress" as the justifying principle of life. This is comparable to Ivan Ilyich's determination to fulfill conventional expectations, to live as others do, to achieve the status and acquire the furnishings other people respect. In his *Confession,* Tolstoy identifies the Paris execution as crucial. It shattered his faith in convention:

When I saw how the head separated from the body, and each separately rattled into its crate, I understood—not in my mind, but my whole being—that no theory of the good sense of Progress, and What Is, can justify this crime, and that if all the people in the world, on whatever theory, from the beginning of the world, should find it necessary—I still knew that it was not necessary but bad. Therefore the judge of what is good and necessary is not what people do and say, and not Progress, but I in my own heart.

The death of his brother Dmitri, Tolstoy says, delivered the second blow to his crumbling faith. Dmitri died in great pain, "not knowing why he lived and even less why he died. No theories could give any answer to these questions, neither to me nor to him." After some fifteen years of married life, from 1862 to 1877, Tolstoy's uncertainties intensified. After the night at Arzamas in 1869, there were further experiences that gathered to a great depression, a fundamental spiritual crisis:

> So I lived, but five years ago something very strange started happening to me. I would get moments—at first of blankness, pauses in life, as though I didn't know how to live, or what I was meant to be doing, and I would get confused and disheartened. But the moments passed, and I would go on as before. Then the blank moments grew more and more frequent and unvaried. And these pauses in life were always expressed in the same words—"For what? And then what?"
>
> At first these just seemed to me to be pointless questions. All this was well known, I thought. If I ever wanted to bother with resolving them, it wouldn't be worth it. Just at the moment there was no time, but as soon as I had time to pause and think, I'd find the answer. And then the questions posed themselves more and more often till, like spots falling always in the same place, all these questions without answers ran together into one big black stain.
>
> What happened to me was the same as what happens to every terminally ill person. At first there appear trivial signs of inadequacy, which the sick person ignores; then the symptoms repeat themselves more and more often and merge into one continuous suffering. The suffering grows, and the invalid has no time to turn before he recognizes that what he took for slight infirmity is the most important thing in all the world, and that is death.

This passage from *A Confession* bears a significant relationship to "The Death of Ivan Ilyich," where the metaphor of sickness is literalized, and Ivan Ilyich's growing sense of spiritual desolation is given a compelling physical cause. Essentially, Ivan Ilyich, in the course of a short mortal illness, recognizes the moral malaise Tolstoy had been fighting for decades.

2

"The Death of Ivan Ilyich" was begun in 1884 and completed in 1886.* Tolstoy's finest parable, "What Men Live By," was written in 1881. The unfinished "Memoirs of a Madman" was begun in 1884. The composition of *A Confession* (1879–1883) overlapped with them all. All four texts throw light on each other.

"Memoirs of a Madman," though presented as fiction, is essentially autobiographical. It describes Tolstoy's experience at Arzamas, a similar night of terror in a Moscow hotel, and a comparable experience lost in the snow when out hunting. Each time, the horror lies in his solitary fear of death and his inability to recognize death's validity: " 'Is this death? I won't have it! Why death? What is it?' " The narrator is an ostensible "madman" who is about to be certified. His lunacy lies in his choice of a radical morality that society thinks crazy—the renunciation of worldly goods for a life of selfless charity (hence the story's first title, "Notes, Not of a Madman"). The ponderous Dostoyevskian irony of the "mad" narrator is unsuited to Tolstoy's habitual simplicity. Moreover, the genuine, and genuinely disturbed episodes at Arzamas and Moscow do not contribute clearly to the story's moral conclusion—the practice of love and charity—even though we can see that logically they are Tolstoy's answer to the horrific futility of life.

Tolstoy illustrates the ideal of love by describing an early episode from the narrator's childhood. His nanny is about to put him into his cot beside his brother, when he demands to climb in by himself. He has an intense sensation of universal harmony. It might be James Joyce or Stanley Spencer speaking:

> I jumped into bed still holding her hand, and then let it go, kicked about under my bedclothes, and wrapped myself up. And I had such a pleasant feeling. I grew quiet and thought: "I love Nurse; Nurse loves me and Mitya; and I love Mitya, and Mitya loves me and Nurse. Nurse loves Taras, and I love Taras, and Mitya loves him. And Taras loves me and Nurse. And

*Chekhov's first volume of short stories was also published in 1886.

Mamma loves me and Nurse, and Nurse loves Mamma and me and Papa—and everybody loves everybody and everybody is happy."

Then suddenly I heard the housekeeper run in and angrily shout something about a sugar basin and Nurse answering indignantly that she had not taken it. And I felt pained, frightened, and horror, cold horror seized me.

This is his first intimation of madness, as his childish faith in universal love is shattered.

In "What Men Live By" Tolstoy transfers the madman's visionary clarity to a more authoritative central figure—Michael, a fallen angel. The story was originally written for children. Irony is replaced by directness. God punishes the angel for disobedience by casting him down to earth, naked and destitute. He is to live as a man till he learns the answer to three fundamental questions.

The angel is taken in by a poor cobbler and his wife, and serves them for seven years. In seven years he smiles three times. The first time comes right at the beginning, when the cobbler's wife is furious with her husband for bringing home this godforsaken down-and-out, the unrecognized angel. She is softened by her husband's rebuke, fetches the outcast a shirt, and gives him soup. The angel later recalls that when the woman was angry with her husband, " 'the spirit of death came from her mouth; I could not speak for the stench of death that spread around her. She wished to drive me out into the cold, and *I knew that if she did so she would die.*' " But when her husband speaks to her of God and she relents, the angel smiles for the first time. " 'I saw that death no longer dwelt in her; she had become alive, and in her, too, I saw God.' "

In "Memoirs of a Madman" a callous world deems charity insane. In "What Men Live By" Tolstoy goes further—life without love is a living death.

———

In "The Death of Ivan Ilyich," the laconic parable of "What Men Live By" is replaced by incontrovertible realism. The story opens with the news of Ivan Ilyich's death. The immediate response of his lawyer colleagues is relief that "he is dead, not I," and pleasant calculations about the promotions consequent on his vacated place. Tolstoy writes from the

point of view of ordinary mankind, whose egotism is natural and immediately recognizable. There is no fallen angel here to tell us this attitude
is deathly, no madman to warn us that this response is the world's folly.
"Well, there you go, he's dead, but I'm not" is a sentiment, as Dr. Johnson
would have said, "to which every bosom returns an echo." And why not?
When Ivan Ilyich's friend Piotr Ivanovich visits the house of mourning,
he turns away from the corpse, with its stern reminder for the living.
"Such a reminder seemed to Piotr Ivanovich to be out of place here, or
at least of no relevance to himself." Throughout the story's first section,
inevitable death is repeatedly ignored. The faint odor of decaying flesh
is dissipated by Gerasim the servant, unobtrusively sprinkling the death
chamber with disinfectant. The mourners, formal respects duly paid,
hasten away to their evening card tables. And yet the inconvenient fact
of death remains—irrepressible as the springs of the ottoman that so
discomfit Piotr Ivanovich as he expresses his condolences to Ivan Ilyich's
widow.

In the remaining narrative Tolstoy makes his readers *inhabit* the
death from which Piotr Ivanovich and the other mourners so assidu-
ously avert their eyes. We live it entirely through Ivan Ilyich's appalled
perceptions, as he sickens, suffers, and dies. Tolstoy forces us to confront
dying head-on—in the way the lady of "Three Deaths" and his own
brother Dmitri writhed against. We watch *it* with the horrified clarity
that has haunted Tolstoy ever since Arzamas.

———

In the eyes of the world, in the eyes of Ivan Ilyich himself, he has had a
successful career—from cheerful child to bright law student; from special assistant to a provincial governor to provincial examining magistrate
of the fifth rank to public prosecutor; from the provinces to Petersburg,
step after orderly step—till, in the blundering words of Nabokov's Pnin,
he "fell and got in consequence kidney of the cancer."

And yet, implicitly, indirectly, Tolstoy shows Ivan Ilyich's smoothly
absorbed progress to be a gradual spiritual death. This is subtly, almost
imperceptibly charted in his diminishing concern for justice and growing appetite for power. It is evident in his scrupulously professional
preference for the efficient administration of general codes over indi-

vidual factors and personal predicaments—his habitual practice "to exclude all the raw, living matter that inevitably clogs the smooth running of official business." With deathly consistency he applies the same principles to his own life, methodically denying every aspect of his own individuality in the pursuit of unimpeachable conformity and the public registers of success. Never has a story dwelt so insistently on "decorum," "high propriety," the "duty...to live a decent life that everyone approved of," "external dignity," "that propriety of external forms required by public opinion" that governs every choice made by Ivan Ilyich. His moral desiccation is even more painfully apparent in his growing coldness, his frank distaste for his quarrelsome wife and daughter, and the deeply unsympathetic lovelessness that intensifies as his illness grows worse.

Thus Ivan Ilyich's shriveled spirit comes to display the aridity Tolstoy experienced at Arzamas, that "painfully dry and spiteful feeling, no atom of kindliness, a dull and steady spitefulness" toward himself and the unfeeling world. The reader coming to "The Death of Ivan Ilyich" with no knowledge of the thoughts and experiences that culminated in its composition may not realize that Ivan Ilyich's dying began long before his illness struck. Tolstoy, however, recognized at Arzamas that "it seems that death is terrible, but...it is one's dying life that is terrible." In his successful years Ivan Ilyich is like the angry cobbler's wife before charity softens her. The smell of death is all around him.

Yet as Ivan Ilyich grows worse physically, his moral degeneration is gradually, barely perceptibly set in reverse. The denial of individuality inherent both in his practice of the law and in his own pursuit of a conventionally decorous life is rudely disturbed by his dawning sense that he is dying, that the dull general rule must also apply to him in all his inestimable singularity. He remembers the syllogism he learned as a boy: "Caius is a man, men are mortal, therefore Caius is mortal." It had always seemed to him correct only in relation to Caius, not to himself. "[H]e was not Caius and not man in general. He was always quite, quite different from all other beings. He was little Vanya with Mamma, with Papa...." All his lost quiddity is captured in one piercing, banal, tragic sentence: "Did Caius know the smell of the striped leather ball Vanya loved so much?" On his sickbed, memories of his earliest years return with increasing frequency. His mind moves from the stewed prunes offered to him at lunch that day to the dried French plums of his childhood—their peculiar flavor and the rush of saliva when he sucked their stones. With these sharply particular memories comes the gradual realization that from that time his life has steadily deteriorated, even as he thought he was doing so well:

> Marriage…so accidental, and then disillusion, and the smell of his wife's breath, and the sensuality and hypocrisy! And that deathly job, and those anxieties about money, and one year like that, and two, and ten, and twenty. Exactly as though I was steadily walking down a mountain, and thinking I was climbing it. And so I was.

However, as illness robs him of physical dignity, the moral drift downhill is gradually reversed. It is striking that Ivan Ilyich's first selfless impulse is prompted by the smell of his night soil, which the young servant Gerasim is about to remove from the sickroom. Robbed of the decorum he sought all his life, weakly collapsed half naked on an armchair, his trousers around his ankles, he apologizes to Gerasim for his unpleasant task. It is his first kindling of humanity. Gerasim's response differs from the politely encouraging lies of Ivan Ilyich's family, doctors, and friends. Later, he is the only one to state the case frankly. What's a little trouble when his master's dying? Such truthfulness comes as a profound relief to Ivan Ilyich, and the informal intimacy between them grows. Gerasim spends many nights patiently sitting with his master, supporting his legs high on his shoulders, which seems to ease the continuous pain.

That literally topsy-turvy scene suggests the inverted relationship evolving between master and servant. In his suffering Ivan Ilyich wants to cry, to be petted and cried over, to be pitied as a sick child is pitied. When his friends come, decorum and old habit force him to suck in his lips and give dry opinions on the latest court judgments. But in Gerasim he can feel the compassion he craves and his unabashed physical dependence is liberating.

Master is subordinated to man, and the judge is condemned to death. When Ivan Ilyich, Public Prosecutor, first consults a celebrated specialist, he is incensed to find the twinkling detachment he himself habitually employed, in passing court judgments on others, turned on himself. Now he is the wretch on trial, and "the doctor made his summing-up just as brilliantly, looking over his spectacles triumphantly and even gaily at the accused." In the last stages of his illness, struggling to reassess his own life, Ivan Ilyich is still unable to recognize that he, who always lived with such scrupulous decorum, could ever have done anything wrong. However, his memory of the usher's cry, "The court is in session!" modulates to an inadvertent admission of guilt: "The judge is coming!...Here he comes, the judge! 'But I'm not to blame!' " And on his very last day, he struggles against the terrifying sensation that he is being bundled into a black sack by an invisible, irresistible force, "as a man condemned to death struggles in the hands of the executioner."

Yet the black bag is both fearful and longed for. Ivan Ilyich suffers less from physical pain than from his revulsion from death—and the simultaneous, apparently unrealizable imperative to give way to it. Tolstoy, at Arzamas, felt "always the same horror...something tearing within that yet could not be torn apart." Ivan Ilyich is "both afraid, and wants to fall through" the sack, "he struggles against it, and he tries to help." Women in labor, I think, sometimes experience something of this difficult yearning to give way to an inevitable physical process, without knowing how to let themselves go, how to set it in motion. In the end, what makes it happen? "He experienced that sensation he sometimes got in a railway carriage, when you think you are moving forward while actually going backward, and suddenly realize your true direction." Then pity finally liberates Ivan Ilyich.

The dying man was still screaming desperately and throwing his arms about. His hand fell on the boy's head. The boy caught hold of it, pressed it to his lips, and burst into tears.

It was just at this point that Ivan Ilyich fell through, saw the glimmer of light, and it became clear to him that his life had not been what it should have been, but that it could still be put right. He asked himself, what is *it,* and fell still, listening. Here he felt someone kissing his hand. He opened his eyes and glanced at his son. He felt sorry for him. His wife came up to him. He glanced at her. She was gazing at him with a look of despair on her face, her mouth open, unwiped tears on her nose and cheeks. He felt sorry for her....

And suddenly it was clear to him that what had been exhausting him and would not leave him was suddenly leaving him, falling away on two sides and ten sides and all sides.

3

Soon after the completion of "The Death of Ivan Ilyich," Tolstoy reflected yet again on his trip to the distant Penza province in search of cheap land, the trip that brought him to unforgettable Arzamas. "How Much Land Does a Man Need?" (1886) is a simple parable in the manner of the fallen-angel narrative of "What Men Live By." The peasant Pahom, by dint of hard work and good management, succeeds in building up a smallholding. The pursuit of more and better land drives him on, beyond the Volga, and finally to the land of the Bashkirs. They offer him a bizarre bargain—they will sell him as much virgin soil as he can encompass on foot in a day. If he fails to return to his starting point before sunset, he loses his money and the land. Inevitably, acquisitiveness undoes him. The grassland here is so lush. The hollow there is just right for flax. He runs faster and faster to ring his territory. As the sun drops below the horizon, his last, desperate spurt up the hill where he started kills him. Six feet by two is all the land a man needs.

The parable is predictable and weakened by supernatural machinery—Pahom's folly is diminished because he is the victim of the Evil One. "How Much Land" is less effective than the longer and more complex "What Men Live By"—though the two stories share a moral. After Michael, the fallen angel, has spent six years working for the cobbler, and his beautiful work is widely known, a rich merchant visits the hovel. He is a huge ox of a man. He demands a pair of boots to be made of the fine leather he provides. They must last a year without mending. The cobbler looks anxiously at Michael to see if he can do the job, but

Michael is gazing into the corner behind the merchant, smiling. The cobbler agrees, the merchant leaves, and Michael sets to work. The cobbler's wife is puzzled to see that he is doing the work all wrong. He has cut the leather round, and is sewing with one end of thread, not two. Instead of high welted boots with whole fronts he makes a pair of soft slippers with single soles, and the fine leather is wasted.* There is a knock at the door. The merchant's servant has returned to change the order. His master died before reaching home; they need slippers for the corpse.

Michael smiled for the second time because he saw his old friend, the angel of death, behind the merchant, and learned the answer to God's second question: Learn what is not given to man. It is not given to man to know his own needs.

"Master and Man" was written a decade later, from 1894 to 1895. Forty years had passed since Tolstoy was lost in the snowstorm at Belogorodtsevskaya. Over thirty had passed since he drove out to the distant Penza province to snap up an easy bargain from some fool who did not understand his own business. Like Tolstoy, Vassili Andreyich Brekhunov, the master, and his man Nikita—and the horse Mukhorty— are lost in a blizzard. Like Tolstoy and like Pahom in "How Much Land Does a Man Need," Vassili Andreyich is impelled on his crazy journey by the determination to buy up land on the cheap. "Insensible of mortality, and desperately mortal,"† like Pahom and the rich merchant of "What Men Live By," Vassili Andreyich does not know his own needs. Finally, Vassili Andreyich discovers that pity dispels the terror of death and, dying himself, saves the life of his servant. Not unlike Ivan Ilyich, who is released into death by pity for his wife and son.

4

"Morality and art," Tolstoy's unabashed response to the execution in Paris, creates difficulties for a sophisticated readership. "We hate poetry

---

*Tolstoy sewed his own boots and writes with authority.
†Shakespeare, *Measure for Measure*, IV.ii.152.

that has a palpable design on us," Keats complained about Wordsworth. Nabokov concurs: "I never could admit that a writer's job was to improve the morals of his country, and point out lofty ideals from the tremendous height of a soapbox." In his best work Tolstoy does not mount a soapbox, yet many readers resent his moralizing. Michael Beresford, the editor of the standard annotated Russian text of "The Death of Ivan Ilyich," writes as if Tolstoy believed in a punitive God: "The reason why all this pain and suffering have been inflicted on Ivan Ilyich [is] that he should come to see the error of the way he has lived and repent." Yet the myth of redemptive suffering, Beresford points out sternly, is open to "serious objections" since "suffering afflicts good men as well as bad" and "pain does not necessarily ennoble men." In his view, Ivan Ilyich "is granted the precious knowledge of love only in extremis, when it is too late for him to put it into practice, except to stutter a few incoherent syllables of forgiveness."

Beresford is wrong. His reading postulates an avenging deity, an authorial alter ego, bent on the infliction of educative suffering on Ivan Ilyich. Tolstoy, on the contrary, points out from the start that Ivan Ilyich's life had been "simple, commonplace, and most terrible." He is not particularly good, nor particularly bad. Ivan Ilyich himself creates the moral deathliness of his life which is finally concretized in his illness. The focus of the story is not on "punishment" but on Ivan Ilyich's response first to life and then to sickness and death. Moreover, Tolstoy is well aware that suffering is destructive as well as redemptive. Everything irritates Ivan Ilyich.

> [H]e could feel his own anger killing him but was unable to restrain himself. You might think he should have realized that his fury against people and circumstances aggravated his illness and consequently he should avoid paying attention to any unpleasantnesses, but his reasoning went the opposite way—he said he needed peace of mind, scrutinized everything that might disrupt his peace of mind, and the slightest disruption infuriated him.

Love is not raised in the story's last pages. It is his wife and son's pity that rouses Ivan Ilyich's reciprocal compassion. His last word, an attempt to say "*prosti*" ("forgive me") is a stumbled apology and not a pardon. Ironically enough, no one understands what he says.

John Bayley, too, dislikes "The Death of Ivan Ilyich," because he finds the story is subordinated to its moral: "Action and outcome are preconceived, and the purpose of the writer is paramount." He objects to Ivan Ilyich's dying sensation of being bundled into a black bag, and his final sense of liberation—on the extraordinary grounds that, "as Tolstoy had obviously experienced neither of these states that he wished upon his character, the ending of 'The Death of Ivan Ilyich' is the supreme example of his conviction that he now knew best about everything." Conversely, perversely, Bayley praises "Master and Man" because "there is no moral, or rather the moral is a highly ambiguous one." Bayley thinks—unaccountably, against the text—that Vassili Andreyich warms his servant in order to warm himself. So "death for the master comes without either terror or meaning."

Bayley is wrong. Vassili Andreyich does not warm Nikita in order to warm himself. True, his hands and feet begin to freeze, "[but] he wasn't thinking of his legs, or his hands; he thought only about how he could warm the peasant lying under him." His death is full of meaning that he understands well:

> He understands that this is death, but this doesn't trouble him either. He remembers that Nikita is lying under him, and that he was warmed and is alive, and it seems to him that he is Nikita and Nikita is he, and that his life is not in himself, but in Nikita. He strains his ears, and hears breathing, and even a light snore, from Nikita. "Nikita is alive, and that means I am living too," he says to himself triumphantly.
>
> And he remembers his money, his shop, his house, his buying and selling, and the Mironov millions, and it is hard for him to understand why that man, whom people called Vassili Brekhunov, troubled himself with all those things that troubled him. "Oh well, he didn't know what it was all about," he thinks, of Vassili Brekhunov. "He didn't know, as now I know...."

As for Bayley's indictment of Tolstoy's arrogance in describing Ivan Ilyich's unknowable sensations at the moment of death—if writers could only describe what they experienced at firsthand, most literature would remain unwritten. Tolstoy's tales of sickness, exposure, and death are germinated by his own experiences. But they are transformed by his powerful, detailed, and supremely realistic imagination.

———

Chekhov wrote to Suvorin,

> You are right to require from the artist a conscious attitude, but you mix up two ideas: *the solution of a problem* and *a correct presentation of the problem*. Only the latter is obligatory for the artist. In *Anna Karenina* and *Onegin* not a single problem is resolved, but they satisfy you completely only because all their problems are correctly presented.

Nothing, though, can stop willful readers from extracting the wrong solution to the problem.

What's more, Chekhov's formulation is not universally applicable. Tolstoy's moral fables—like "What Men Live By" and "How Much Land Does a Man Need"—do set out to pose problems and provide answers. James Joyce thought that "How Much Land Does a Man Need" was "the greatest story that the literature of the world knows." In "What Men Live By," the solutions the fallen angel Michael finds to God's three fundamental questions are extraordinarily satisfying. Like the Ancient Mariner's wedding guest, we listen like a three years' child, and our wish for a moral is candidly and profoundly answered.

Many English and American kindergartens have a weekly session called Show and Tell. The children bring their treasures, show them to the class, and talk about them. In his parables, Tolstoy shows and tells. In great stories like "Master and Man" and "The Death of Ivan Ilyich" he shows more and tells less. Detail wins our conviction. Conviction drives us to share the characters' experiences. And the art is moral when it evokes a moral response. Gradually, reluctantly, we are appalled by Ivan Ilyich's deathly aridity. We suffer with him in his miserable sickness. And we are hugely relieved when at last he recognizes his son's pity, and pities him. We watch with increasing horror each time the master Vassili Andreyich rejects the offer of shelter because business calls, and drives out yet again into the storm. We are disgusted when, in a final paroxysm of selfishness, he flings himself belly down across Mukhorty's back and rides off into the blizzard, leaving Nikita to die. We feel for him and with him when, lying on Nikita, warming him, his jaw trembles, something chokes his throat, and the tears come.

———

Not all artists want to evoke a moral response. Tolstoy does. But note his curious formulation—"Morality and art. I know, I love, and I can" (his diary entry after the execution in Paris). There is love in Tolstoy's extraordinary capacity for universal empathy. He is the artistic equivalent of the peasant Nikita, who talks companionably to everyone and everything—the chickens squawking in the rafters, the intelligent horse Mukhorty, even his belt as he draws it tight.

Turgenev describes a happy visit to Tolstoy one summer. After lunch they went out with the children, sat on the seesaw together, and then wandered over to a tethered horse. Tolstoy stroked it, whispering in its cocked ear, and told them what it was thinking. "I could have listened for ever," Turgenev said. "He had got inside the very soul of the poor beast and taken me with him." Likewise, Tolstoy's affection was roused by the baggage horse that laid back its ears and tried to overtake his sledge at Belogorodtsevskaya. And so it is that Mukhorty is as fully realized as the human beings in "Master and Man."

———

Early in his career, in the Sevastopol sketches he wrote when fighting in the Crimea, Tolstoy set out an early version of his artistic credo.

> Where in this tale is the evil that should be avoided, and where the good that should be imitated? Who is the villain and who the hero of the story? All are good and all are bad ...
>
> The hero of my tale—whom I love with all the power of my soul, whom I have tried to portray in all his beauty, who has been, is, and will be beautiful—is Truth.

The Sevastopol sketches were noticed and admired by Tsar Alexander II. They were also censored. *A Confession* was banned in Russia. In 1901

Tolstoy was excommunicated by the Holy Synod of the Russian Orthodox Church. Perhaps the narrator of "Memoirs of a Madman" was right—and Tolstoy's beliefs were folly to the world.

———

ANN PASTERNAK SLATER, Fellow and Tutor in English at St. Anne's College, Oxford, was brought up bilingually in Russian and English by her mother, the sister of Boris Pasternak. She has written and lectured on Pasternak's translations of Shakespeare, and is the translator of his brother Alexander Pasternak's memoirs, *A Vanished Present* (1984). Her grandfather Leonid Pasternak was Tolstoy's friend and one of his first illustrators, working with him on *War and Peace, Resurrection,* and the late short story "What Men Live By."

Translator's Note

Tolstoy's style is simple and direct—famously so.

This is not entirely true. In both these stories there are many passages where the syntax is clumsy. There is much repetition. This is a literal translation of a passage from "Master and Man" (page 100):

> The thought came to him that he might, and very probably would, die that night, but this thought didn't seem particularly unpleasant to him, nor particularly frightening. The thought didn't seem to him to be particularly unpleasant because his whole life hadn't been a perpetual holiday, but on the contrary an uninterrupted round of hard labor, which was beginning to tire him. Nor was the thought particularly frightening because, apart from the masters he served here, like Vassili Andreyich, in this life he always felt himself dependent on the main master, the one who sent him into this life, and he knew that even in death he would stay in this master's power, and this master would not treat him badly.

Often, but not always, there is a literary justification for the repetition of single words.

> The corpse lay with that particular ponderousness common to all corpses, the dead limbs sunken in their corpse-like way deep in the lining of the coffin, the head bowed forever on its pillow, displaying—prominently, as

corpses always do—a waxy yellow forehead.... ("The Death of Ivan Ilyich," p. 6, literal translation)

Since the root of the Russian adjective "dead" is the same as that of the noun "corpse," the original text is even more repetitive. The dead weight of the dead is laid on with a deliberately heavy hand. Or again, when Ivan Ilyich is distracted from his legal duties by anxieties about his health:

He went into his study and promptly sat down to his *files*. He read them, worked at them, but the consciousness that he had postponed an important, intimate *business* he would deal with as soon as he finished, did not leave him. When he finished his *papers*, he remembered that this intimate *business* was to think about his blind gut. (p. 34)

For each of the italicized variants, the Russian text has the single word *delo*, meaning specific "files," "business," and "work" in general. Even in linguistic terms, Ivan Ilyich's physical preoccupations are taking over his professional duties.

In a couple of instances, the repetition of a single phrase seems to emphasize a significant glissando in sense, which I have identified in the Notes (see pp. 113–14, notes 36, 38). In general, I have tried to maintain as lucid, emphatic, and direct a style as possible, diminishing the repetition and clarifying syntactical clumsiness where I felt it was not serving a perceptible purpose.

The first quotation from "Master and Man" illustrates another peculiarity of Tolstoy's late style. It has a repetitive, circular ruminativeness which could almost be called authorial stream of consciousness. The narrator appears to be thinking aloud. Very often this objective narrative shifts imperceptibly to a character's subjective impressions. Here is Ivan Ilyich preparing his new home in Petersburg. The passage begins in traditional, factual third-person narrative: "Ivan Ilyich oversaw everything himself: he chose the wallpaper, bought more furniture." Then it shifts to his thoughts: "Falling asleep, he imagined the reception room as it would become. Looking into the still unfinished sitting room, he envisaged the fireplace, the fire screen...." The language tracing his thoughts becomes progressively suffused with his own idiolect: "The thought of how he would amaze Pasha and Lizanka, who also had taste in these matters, made him glad." Pasha and Lizanka are affectionate diminutives for Ivan Ilyich's wife and daughter. These diminutives appear uniquely here, when Ivan Ilyich's feelings toward them are softened. Elsewhere, the narrative never refers to them by these names. And no one but Ivan Ilyich thinks that he, or his wife and daughter, have "taste in these things." Certainly the main tenor of the objective narrative is that Ivan Ilyich's new home is tastelessly conventional. But by now we are deep in Ivan Ilyich's thoughts, as the present tense of the next sentence demonstrates: "They can't possibly expect all this." This is Ivan Ilyich thinking aloud to himself. And yet the text is unmarked by any explanatory quotation marks to distinguish his subjective thoughts from the objective narrative. Tolstoy is dipping in and out of free indirect discourse, *style indirecte libre*.

This narrative flexibility of tone is one of the great pleasures of "The Death of Ivan Ilyich." It occurs less frequently in "Master and Man." And, regrettably, it is usually smoothed away in translation. Certainly the unexpected shifts of tense and person can be startling. Take the following passage, describing Ivan Ilyich's recreations, beginning in objective third-person narrative, shifting to his own voice in reported speech, marked by his clichés, and ending in the unabashed, subjective first person:

> His professional pleasures were the pleasures of self-esteem, his social pleasures were the pleasures of vanity, but Ivan Ilyich's real pleasure was the pleasure of playing vint. He used to admit that after everything, after whatever unpleasantnesses might have happened during his day, the one pleasure that shone like a candle, brighter than all others, was the prospect of sitting down with good players, poker-faced partners, to play vint, in a party of four of course (it's really unpleasant sitting out if there are five of you, even if you pretend oh, I love it).... (pp. 24–25)

Tolstoy is like D. H. Lawrence—on occasion astonishingly repetitive, frequently clumsy. Both allow the thoughts of their characters to suffuse an apparently objective narrative. Unlike the controlled exploitation of free indirect discourse in, say, Joyce's *Dubliners*, what we find in both Tolstoy and Lawrence is the instinctive imaginative projection of the sympathetic author. In spite of the apparent roughness of the unexpected shifts in person and tense, I have done my best to preserve this quality in Tolstoy's texts.

Everything else is more or less routine. I have simplified the transliteration of Russian names for the reader's sake, and tried to clarify things a little in "Master and Man," where the servant Nikita is often called "Mikita" and even "Mikit" in the dialogue (a Ukrainian variant of the name). In this story, much of the peasants' dialogue is enriched by malapropisms for which I was unable to find plausible English equivalents. Nikita's "brigle" for "bridle" sounded silly and looked like a misprint. Uniquely Russian objects like *valenki* (felt boots) are annotated, and measurements have been modernized.

I have benefited from the great translations of Constance Garnett, Louise and Aylmer Maude—and Henry Bergen, whose forgotten translation of "Master and Man," published as a sixpenny pamphlet in the "Simple Life" series in 1904, is not merely a fine translation but a bibliographic curio, having some sizeable omissions and additions not found in the standard Russian texts of this story.

The Court in Session by Leonid Pasternak (1862–1945).

THE DEATH OF IVAN ILYICH

During a break in the hearing of the Melvinski case in the great hall of the Law Courts, members of the judicial council and the public prosecutor met in Ivan Yegorovich Shebek's private chambers. The conversation turned to the famous Krasov affair. Feodor Vassilievich grew heated demonstrating that it was not subject to jurisdiction. Ivan Yegorovich held his own. Piotr Ivanovich, who had not participated initially, took no part in the argument and leafed through the newly delivered *Gazette*.

"Gentlemen!" he said, "Ivan Ilyich is dead."

"Not really?"

"Here; read it for yourself," he said to Feodor Vassilievich, passing him the fresh sheets, still with their own smell.

The black-framed notice ran: "It is with deep regret that Praskovya Feodorovna Golovina informs relatives and friends of the death of her beloved husband, Ivan Ilyich Golovin, Member of the Court of Justice, on February the fourth of this year, 1882. The body will be laid to rest on Friday at 1 P.M."

Ivan Ilyich was a colleague of the gentlemen present, and everyone liked him. He had been ill for several weeks; people said the disease was incurable. His place had been kept open for him, but it was generally assumed that, were he to die, Alexeyev might get his place, and Alexeyev's place would be taken either by Vinnikov or Shtabel. So when they heard of the death of Ivan Ilyich, the first thought of all those present in Shebek's chambers was how this might affect their own relocations and promotions, and those of their friends.

"Now I'll probably get Shtabel's place or Vinnikov's," thought Feodor Vassilievich. "It's been promised to me for a long time. The promotion will bring me a raise of eight hundred rubles, apart from the allowance for office expenses."[1]

"I'll have to put in for my brother-in-law's transfer from Kaluga," thought Piotr Ivanovich. "My wife will be very pleased. And then no one can say I never did anything for her relatives."

"I thought he'd never get up from his bed again," said Piotr Ivanovich aloud. "Very sad."

"What exactly was wrong with him?"

"The doctors couldn't make it out. That is, they could, but each one thought something different. The last time I saw him, I thought he'd get better."

"And I didn't manage to visit him after the holidays. I kept meaning to go."

"Did he have property?"

"I think something very small came to him through his wife. But really quite insignificant."

"Yes, we'll have to pay our respects. They lived a dreadfully long way out."

"A long way from you, you mean. Everything's a long way from you."

"He just can't forgive my living beyond the river," said Piotr Ivanovich, smiling at Shebek. The conversation passed to the distances between different parts of the city, and they went back into court.

Apart from the considerations prompted by this death—the changes of post and possible permutations at work that were its probable consequences—the fact of a near acquaintance dying evoked in everyone who heard about it the happy feeling that he is dead, not I.

"Well, there you go, he's dead, but I'm not," each of them thought. And close acquaintances, the so-called friends of Ivan Ilyich, involuntarily found themselves also thinking that now they would have to go through the tedious round of social duties, driving out to the funeral and paying their condolences to the widow.

The closest of all were Feodor Vassilievich and Piotr Ivanovich.

Piotr Ivanovich had been Ivan Ilyich's friend from their time at law school[2] together, and felt under an obligation to him.

At lunchtime he told his wife about Ivan Ilyich's death and the possibility of his brother-in-law's transfer to their circle. Forgoing his usual after-dinner nap, he put on his tails and drove out to the Golovins.

A carriage and two cabs stood at the entrance to Ivan Ilyich's apartment. In the entrance hall downstairs, propped against the wall by the coat stand, was the coffin lid, draped in silk, decorated with tassels and burnished gold braid. Two ladies in black were taking off their furs. He knew one of them, the sister of Ivan Ilyich, but the other was a stranger. Schwartz, a colleague, was on his way downstairs. Glimpsing Piotr Ivanovich as he entered, Schwartz stopped and winked at him from the top step, suggesting, as it were, "Ivan Ilyich has made a real mess of things, not like you and me."

Schwartz's face with its English side-whiskers, and indeed his entire figure, slim in evening dress, wore its usual air of elegant solemnity—a solemnity which was constantly contradicted by Schwartz's jocular character, acquiring a particular piquancy in the present setting. Or so Piotr Ivanovich thought.

Piotr Ivanovich allowed the ladies to pass before him and followed them slowly upstairs. Schwartz did not come down but waited at the top. Piotr Ivanovich understood why: he wanted to arrange where they would play cards that evening. The ladies went through to visit the widow, and Schwartz, with tight, serious mouth and a playful glance, inclined his head, motioning Piotr Ivanovich to the right, the room where the corpse was laid out.

Piotr Ivanovich entered, as one always does, in total uncertainty over what he should do when he got there. But one thing was quite clear—there can be no harm in crossing yourself in such circumstances. Because he was not certain whether you should bow at the same time, he chose to compromise: he began crossing himself and inclining his head slightly. At the same time he was taking in the room, so far as the movement of his hands and head allowed. Two young men, one a schoolboy—the nephews, probably—were coming out of the room, crossing themselves. An old lady was standing motionless. And a woman with strangely raised eyebrows was whispering something to her. A hearty church deacon[3] in a frock coat was reading something loudly and resolutely, in a way that left no room for contradiction. Gerasim, the peasant who normally waited at table, passed in front of Piotr Ivanovich with a light step, strewing something over the floor. Seeing this, Piotr

Ivanovich immediately caught the slight smell of decomposition. The last time Piotr Ivanovich had visited Ivan Ilyich, he had seen Gerasim in the sick room. He had taken on the duties of a nurse, and Ivan Ilyich was particularly fond of him. Piotr Ivanovich kept on crossing himself and bowing slightly to an indeterminate point somewhere between the coffin, the deacon, and the icons on the table in the corner. Then, when the movement of his hand crossing himself seemed to have gone on altogether too long, he paused and began looking at the corpse.

The dead man lay with that particular ponderousness common to all corpses, the dead limbs sunken deep in the lining of the coffin, the head bowed forever on its pillow, displaying—prominently, as the dead always do—a waxy yellow forehead with bald patches on the sunken brow, and a pendulous nose seemingly compressing the upper lip. He had grown much thinner and was considerably changed since Piotr Ivanovich last saw him, but his face, as with all the dead, was more beautiful and, more important than that, more meaningful than it had been in his lifetime. The expression on the face suggested that what needed to be done had been done, and done as it should be. Moreover, the expression held a rebuke or a reminder to the living. Such a reminder seemed to Piotr Ivanovich to be out of place here, or at least of no relevance to him. He became rather uncomfortable, somehow. He hastily crossed himself again—too quickly, it seemed to him, without due regard for the appropriate courtesies, and turned to leave. Schwartz was waiting for him in the next room, his legs set wide, his hands behind his back playing with his top hat. One look at Schwartz's playful, neat, and elegant figure refreshed Piotr Ivanovich. He realized that Schwartz rose above such things and did not succumb to unpleasant impressions. His mere appearance proclaimed: the incident of the present obsequies cannot, in any way, serve as an adequate reason for the order of the session to be disrupted—that is, nothing can stop a new pack of cards being unwrapped and shuffled this very evening, while the footman sets out four fresh candles; there are, in short, no grounds for thinking that this episode can stop us spending this evening as pleasantly as any other evening. Schwartz even whispered this to Piotr Ivanovich as he went past, suggesting he should join the company at Feodor Vassilievich's. But evidently it was not ordained that Piotr Ivanovich should play cards that evening. Praskovya Feodorovna came out of her quarters. She was a short, fat woman, whose figure grew progressively wider from head to foot, despite her attempts to achieve the opposite—dressed all in black, her head veiled in lace, and her eyebrows arched in the same peculiar manner as the other lady standing by the coffin. She was leading the other ladies to the room where the body lay, with the words, "The funeral will begin in a moment; please go through."

Schwartz paused, bowing ambiguously, neither visibly accepting nor refusing her invitation. Praskovya Feodorovna recognized Piotr Ivanovich, sighed, came directly to him, took him by the hand, and said, "I know that you were a true friend to Ivan Ilyich...." She was looking at him in expectation of an appropriate response.

Piotr Ivanovich knew that, just as it had been correct to cross himself there, so it was proper to press her hand here, to sigh, and say, "Believe me..." Accordingly, he did so. And, having done so, felt that he had achieved the desired result, that he was moved, and so was she.

"Come with me, before they start in there; I must have a word with you," said the widow. "Give me your arm."

Piotr Ivanovich gave her his arm, and they went into the inner room, passing Schwartz, who winked mournfully at Piotr Ivanovich. "So much for our card game! Don't be offended if we find someone else. Five can always play, if you manage to get away," said his playful glance.

Piotr Ivanovich sighed even more deeply and despondently, and Praskovya Feodorovna pressed his hand gratefully. They entered her dimly lit sitting room, upholstered in pink cretonne, and sat down by a table—she on a divan, Piotr Ivanovich on a low ottoman, whose broken springs yielded unpredictably to his weight. Praskovya Feodorovna wanted to warn him that he should sit somewhere else, but thought such a warning inappropriate to her present circumstances and changed her mind. Sitting down on the ottoman, Piotr Ivanovich remembered Ivan Ilyich furnishing the room and asking his advice about this same pink cretonne with its pattern of green leaves. On her way to the divan, the widow passed an occasional table (the room was full of furniture and knickknacks), and the black lace of her mantilla caught on its carvings.

Piotr Ivanovich half rose to unhook it, and the liberated ottoman heaved under him and gave him a shove. The widow began unhitching the lace herself. Piotr Ivanovich sat down again, crushing the rebellious springs. But the widow had not freed herself completely. Piotr Ivanovich rose to his feet again, and the ottoman bounced back with a twang. When all this was over, she took out a clean cambric handkerchief and began crying. However, the business with the lace and the contretemps with the ottoman had cooled Piotr Ivanovich. He sat, looking sullen. This uncomfortable situation was interrupted by the entry of Sokolov, Ivan Ilyich's butler, who announced that the plot in the cemetery ordered by Praskovya Feodorovna would cost two hundred rubles. She stopped crying and, with a martyred look at Piotr Ivanovich, said in French that it was very difficult for her. Piotr Ivanovich made a silent gesture indicating his incontrovertible conviction that it could not be otherwise.

"Do smoke," she said in a magnanimous yet crushed voice, and turned to discuss the price of the plot with Sokolov. Piotr Ivanovich lit up and listened to her minutely questioning the butler about the different plot prices and deciding on the right one. When that had been dealt with, she turned to the fees for the choir. Sokolov left.

"I have to do everything myself," she said to Piotr Ivanovich, moving to one side the albums lying on the table and, noticing that his cigarette ash threatened her table, promptly passed him an ashtray. "I find it mere affectation to protest that my grief prevents me from dealing with practical matters. On the contrary, if anything could console me . . . or at least distract me, it is the arrangements concerning him." She took out her handkerchief again, as though on the point of tears, and suddenly, as if mastering herself, gave a little shake and started speaking calmly. "However, I have something I must discuss with you."

Piotr Ivanovich bowed, repressing the ebullient ottoman springs, which immediately began to stir under him.

"He suffered dreadfully in his last days."

"Dreadfully?" asked Piotr Ivanovich.

"Oh, it was terrible! In the last hours, let alone minutes, he didn't stop screaming for a second. For three days on end he screamed without stopping. It was unbearable. I can't understand how I survived it; he could be heard three rooms off, even with the doors closed. My God, how I suffered!"

"Surely he wasn't conscious?" asked Piotr Ivanovich.

"Yes, he was," she whispered, "to the very last minute. He took his leave of us a quarter of an hour before he died, and even asked us to take Volodya out."

Piotr Ivanovich forgot his uncomfortable awareness of his and her hypocrisy. He remembered this man, whom he had known so well as a cheerful child, a schoolboy, and a colleague, and was suddenly appalled by the thought of his suffering. He saw once more that brow, that nose pressed to the upper lip, and felt frightened for himself.

"Three days of appalling suffering, and death. Why, it could happen to me, too, at any time, even now," he thought. For a moment he was terrified. But, he hardly knew how, the usual thoughts promptly came to his aid—that this had happened to Ivan Ilyich, not himself; that this neither could nor should happen to him; and that thinking such thoughts would only mean succumbing to gloom, which was not good for you, as Schwartz demonstrated. And, having followed this train of thought, Piotr Ivanovich grew calm and started eliciting the facts of Ivan Ilyich's decease with interest, as though death were an experience proper only to Ivan Ilyich and not in the least to himself.

After some remarks about the really dreadful physical suffering endured by Ivan Ilyich (Piotr Ivanovich could find out only those details which affected Praskovya Feodorovna's nervous disposition), the widow evidently decided it was time to get down to business.

"Oh, Piotr Ivanovich, it is so hard, so dreadfully hard, so dreadfully hard." And she started crying again.

Piotr Ivanovich sighed and waited for her to blow her nose. When she had blown her nose, he said, "Believe me…" and she started talking again, finally broaching what had evidently been her main business with him—how she could get money out of the Treasury on her husband's death. She made a show of asking Piotr Ivanovich for advice about her widow's pension, but he could see she already knew more than he did, down to the smallest detail, about everything that could be wrung out of the Treasury. She really wanted to know whether there was any way of extracting anything further. Piotr Ivanovich tried to think up some other strategies, but, having given it a little thought and for politeness's sake criticized the meanness of the government, he said he thought nothing more could be done. Then she sighed, palpably looking now for a way to get rid of her visitor. Realizing this, he extinguished his cigarette, rose, shook her hand, and went into the hall.

In the dining room with the clock that had so pleased Ivan Ilyich when he bought it in an antique shop, Piotr Ivanovich met the priest and some other acquaintances who had driven up for the funeral, and saw a familiar, beautiful young woman, the daughter of Ivan Ilyich. She was dressed in black. Her narrow waist seemed even narrower. She had a gloomy, decided, almost angry expression. She bowed to Piotr Ivanovich as though he were somehow to blame. Behind the daughter stood another figure familiar to Piotr Ivanovich, a wealthy young man with the same offended expression—an examining magistrate who was her fiancé, as Piotr Ivanovich had heard. He bowed wanly to them both and wanted to pass through to the room where the dead man lay, when the small figure of the schoolboy son, dreadfully like his father, appeared on the stair. This was a miniature Ivan Ilyich just as Piotr Ivanovich remembered him in law school. His eyes were tearstained and had that impure look[4] found in boys of thirteen and fourteen. Seeing Piotr Ivanovich, the boy frowned bashfully and severely. Piotr Ivanovich nodded to him and went into the dead man's room. The funeral started—candles, groans, incense, tears, sobbing. Piotr Ivanovich stood with furrowed brow, staring at the feet in front of him. He didn't look at the corpse once, resisted any impulse of emotional weakness to the very end, and was one of the first to leave. There was no one in the hall. Gerasim, the servant, popped out of the dead man's room, rummaged with strong hands through all the furs to find Piotr Ivanovich's coat, and held it out for him.

"Well, Gerasim?" said Piotr Ivanovich, for the sake of saying something. "It's sad, isn't it?"

"God's will. We'll all come to that," said Gerasim, showing his white, even, peasant's teeth, and, like a man caught up by many duties, briskly threw open the door, shouted for the coachman, helped Piotr Ivanovich up, and sprang back to the porch as though preoccupied with his next task.

Piotr Ivanovich was particularly glad of the fresh air after the smells of incense, carbolic acid, and the corpse.

"Where to?" asked the coachman.

"It's not late. I'll call on Feodor Vassilievich."

And Piotr Ivanovich drove off. He found them finishing the first rubber, so it was quite convenient for him to make a fifth in the game.

2

The past history of Ivan Ilyich's life was simple, commonplace, and most terrible.

Ivan Ilyich died when he was forty-five years old, a member of the Court of Justice. He was the son of a civil servant who had made a career for himself in Petersburg working in various ministries and departments. It was the kind of career that brings people to a position where they cannot be fired because of their long service and high rank, although they are clearly incapable of assuming any real responsibilities. So they are found fictional functions, with unfictional salaries of six to ten thousand rubles a year on which they live to a great age.

Such a man was Privy Councillor[5] Ilya Yefimovich Golovin, unnecessary member of various unnecessary departments.

He had three sons. The eldest son had a career similar to his father's but in a different ministry, and was fast approaching that point in his service that brought with it—through sheer inertia—a salary for life. The third son was a failure. He ruined his prospects in various posts and was now working on the railways, and his father and brothers, and particularly their wives, not only disliked meeting him but avoided even remembering his existence except in extreme necessity. The sister married Baron Greff, a Petersburg civil servant like his father-in-law. Ivan Ilyich was *le phénix de la famille*,[6] as they used to say. He was not as chilly and proper as his elder brother, nor as reckless as the younger. He was the midpoint between them—bright, lively, a pleasant and respectable man. He was educated along with his younger brother in the School of Jurisprudence. The younger brother did not complete his education and was expelled in the fifth grade, but Ivan Ilyich finished creditably. Even at school he was what he remained for the rest of his life—talented, likable, cheerfully sociable, but always strictly fulfilling what he felt to be his duties. And his duties were what he thought everyone in authority over him considered to be his duties. He was not a sycophant as a child nor as a grown man, but from his earliest years was drawn—as a fly to bright light—to those in the highest circles, learned from their example, echoed their ideas about life, and established friendly relations with them. All the enthusiasms of his childhood and youth passed away leaving barely a trace; he was sensuous and vain and, toward the end of his school years, acquired liberal views, but always within well-established parameters clearly identified by his instinct for correctness.

There were some things he did while he was at the School of Jurisprudence that had previously seemed pretty despicable to him and aroused a strong sense of self-loathing in him at the time. Subsequently, seeing comparable behavior in people of the highest standing who thought nothing of it, he began to feel that what he had done was not exactly good, but was certainly not worth remembering, and he felt no mortification when it did come to mind.

When Ivan Ilyich graduated from the School of Jurisprudence he was qualified for the tenth class in the civil service. His father provided funds for his outfit. He ordered himself clothes from Scharmer's, hung a medallion on his watch chain inscribed with the words *respice finem,* took leave of his tutor and the prince who was patron of the law school, dined with his friends at Donon's,[7] and with a fashionable new trunk, packed with linen, suits, shaving and toilet sets, and a rug, all ordered and bought from the best suppliers, left for one of the provinces, where his father had obtained a place for him as the Governor's special assistant.

In the province Ivan Ilyich immediately arranged as easy and pleasant a life for himself as he had enjoyed at law school. He did his job, pursued his career, and at the same time indulged himself pleasantly and decorously. Occasionally he was sent on official business to country districts, where he behaved with dignity to high and low alike, maintaining a precise and incorruptible integrity on which he could not help priding himself, fulfilling the tasks entrusted to him, chiefly in connection with the affairs of the Old Believers.[8]

In spite of his youth and predisposition for lighthearted amusement, in official business he was extraordinarily reserved, formal, and even stern, but in a social setting he was often playful, witty, always good-humored, correct and *bon enfant*,[9] as his employer and his employer's wife said of him. For them, he was part of the family.

There was also a liaison with one of the ladies who attached herself to the fashionable young lawyer; there was a milliner; there were drinking parties with visiting cavalry officers and visits to a certain street in the suburbs after dinner; there was, too, servility to his employer and even his employer's wife. But all this was carried with such a tone of high propriety that none of it could be given a bad name: it all fell under the French saying, *il faut que jeunesse se passe*.[10] Everything was done with clean hands in laundered shirts and embellished with French terms—and, above all, in the best possible company and consequently with the approval of the very best people.

Ivan Ilyich spent five years in this service, and then a change came. New legal institutions were created, and new men were needed.

And Ivan Ilyich became the new man.

He was offered the post of examining magistrate,[11] and took it, even though the post was in a different province and he had to abandon the relationships he had built up and create new ones. Ivan Ilyich's friends came to see him off, a group photograph was taken, they presented him with a silver cigarette case, and he left for his new assignment.

Ivan Ilyich the examining magistrate was just as decent and comme il faut[12] as Ivan Ilyich the Governor's assistant, just as good at separating official duties from his personal life, and just as adept at arousing widespread respect. The actual work of examining magistrate was much more attractive and interesting for him. In his previous post he had enjoyed wearing his uniform from Scharmer's, strolling past anxious petitioners and official functionaries waiting for an audience, who enviously watched him going straight to the Governor's office to have tea and a cigarette with him—but there were very few people who depended directly on his authority. There were only the chiefs of police and the Old Believers, when he was sent on special assignments to the rural districts. He liked to deal in a courteous and even comradely manner with these people, who did depend on him; he liked to let them feel that here he was, treating them simply and amicably when it was in his power to crush them. At that time there were few such people. But now, as examining magistrate, Ivan Ilyich felt that everyone, everyone without exception, the most important and self-satisfied people, all of them lay in his power. He need only write certain words on a sheet of paper with an official letterhead, and this important, self-satisfied person will be brought to him as witness or accused, and if Ivan Ilyich chooses not to ask him to sit down, he will have to stand before him to answer his questions. Ivan Ilyich never abused his power; on the contrary, he tried to soften the way it was expressed, but the consciousness of this power and the possibility of softening it constituted the main interest and pleasure of his new post. In his actual work, that is, in the preliminary investigations, Ivan Ilyich very quickly mastered the knack of setting aside all considerations irrelevant to the official aspects of the case, reducing the most complicated matters to a formula in which only the external aspects were recorded, his personal opinion was strictly excluded, and, above all, the due formalities were observed. This was all new. And he was one of the first to apply the reformed Code of 1864[13] in practice.

When he moved to the new town to take up his post as examining magistrate, Ivan Ilyich found himself new friends, made new contacts, established himself afresh, and assumed a slightly different manner. He set himself at a certain dignified distance from the provincial authorities, and selected the best circle among the legal and wealthy gentry living in the town. He affected a tone of light dissatisfaction with the government, moderate liberalism, and civilized public spirit. At the same time, without changing the elegance of his toilet in any way, in his new role Ivan Ilyich stopped shaving his chin and allowed his beard to grow as it pleased.

Ivan Ilyich's life settled into just as happy a pattern in the new town. His chosen circle, which was in opposition to the Governor, was friendly and the company was good. His salary was larger, and whist, which he now started to play, brought considerable pleasure into his life. Ivan Ilyich had the gift of playing cards good-humoredly, quickly and shrewdly assessing his hand, so that in general he was always the winner.

After two years' service in the new town, Ivan Ilyich met his future wife. Praskovya Feodorovna Mikhel was the most attractive, intelligent, brilliant girl in the circle frequented by Ivan Ilyich. Among the other pleasurable distractions from the labors of examining magistrate Ivan Ilyich established a light, playful relationship with Praskovya Feodorovna.

As the Governor's special assistant Ivan Ilyich had danced; as examining magistrate this became an exception. Now his dancing implied—although I administer the reformed Code and rank fifth grade in the civil service, if it comes to dancing, watch me prove I can do that better than anyone else, too. So at the end of an evening he occasionally danced with Praskovya Feodorovna and it was mainly during these dances that he won her. She fell in love with him. Ivan Ilyich did not have a clear and distinct intention to marry, but when the girl fell in love with him, he considered the question. "And, really, why shouldn't I marry?" he said to himself.

The young lady came from good aristocratic stock. She was not unattractive. She brought a small property with her. Ivan Ilyich could have counted on a more dazzling match, but even this was not a bad one. He had his salary. She, he hoped, would have as much. Her birth was good. She was sweet, pretty, and eminently respectable. To say that he married because he fell in love with his fiancée and found in her an answering echo to his own view of life would be as inaccurate as to say that he married because the people in his circle approved of the match. He married for both reasons: he was pleasing himself by taking such a wife, and at the same time he was doing what his superiors thought the right thing to do.

And Ivan Ilyich married.

The very process of getting married, and the beginning of married life—with its marital caresses, new furniture, new crockery, new linen—passed very happily until his wife's pregnancy. Ivan Ilyich even began to think that, far from wedlock upsetting his light, pleasant, gay manner of life, his marriage would actually intensify this congenial state of affairs—always respectable and popularly respected, the qualities Ivan Ilyich thought natural to life in general. But from the first months of his wife's pregnancy, something new emerged. It was so unexpected and unpleasant, so burdensome and unseemly, it could hardly have been predicted and was impossible to ignore.

For no evident reason, as it seemed to Ivan Ilyich—*de gaîté de cœur*,[14] as he said to himself—his wife began disrupting the ease and propriety of his life. For no reason at all she became jealous, demanded his attentions, found fault with everything, and made rude, disagreeable scenes.

At first Ivan Ilyich hoped to free himself from this unpleasant situation by the same light, proper response to life that had served him well in the past. He tried to ignore his wife's moods, continued to live as lightly and pleasantly as before; he invited friends to his home to make up a hand of cards and tried to go out to his club or to visit his friends. But on one occasion his wife began to abuse him in such coarse language, with such energy and with such persistent aggression that Ivan Ilyich was appalled. She had evidently decided not to give up until he submitted—that is, until he stayed at home and was as dull as she was. He realized that the married state, at any rate with his wife, was not always conducive to the pleasures and proprieties of life, but, on the contrary, often disrupted them; for this reason it was imperative that he should protect himself from such disturbances. And Ivan Ilyich began searching out the means to achieve this. His official duties were the one thing that made some impression on Praskovya Feodorovna, and through his official duties and the responsibilities arising from them Ivan Ilyich began his struggle with his wife to stake out his independent world.

With the birth of the child, the attempts to feed it and the various failures to do so, with the real and imagined illnesses of mother and child, all of which demanded his participation but none of which were in the least comprehensible to him, Ivan Ilyich's need to create his own space outside the family became even more imperative.

The more irritating and demanding his wife became, the more Ivan Ilyich transferred the center of gravity of his life to his official duties, and the more ambitious he became.

Very soon, not longer than a year after his marriage, Ivan Ilyich understood that matrimony, while offering some conveniences in life, was in fact a very complicated and difficult matter and that, in order to fulfill his duty—that is, to lead a decent life that everyone approved of—he must work out a definite approach to married life, just as he had done for his official life.

And Ivan Ilyich worked out an approach to married life. He asked no more of it than the conveniences which it was able to provide—dinner at home, a housewife, and a bed, and, above all, that propriety of external forms required by public opinion. For the rest, he looked for pleasure and good cheer, and when he found them, was very grateful. If, on the contrary, he met with antagonism and querulousness, he immediately retreated into his palisaded world of work and found his pleasure there.

Ivan Ilyich was valued as a good colleague, and after three years was made assistant public prosecutor. The new duties, their importance, the power to bring anyone to trial and imprison him, the public attention his speeches received, the success Ivan Ilyich enjoyed in this capacity—all this attracted him further to his employment.

More children came. His wife became even more querulous and bad tempered, but the approach Ivan Ilyich had evolved to family life made him almost impervious to her scenes.

After seven years' service in the same town Ivan Ilyich was transferred to a different province to take up the post of public prosecutor. They moved; money was short; and his wife took an aversion to the place where they were stationed. Although his salary was slightly higher, life was more expensive, and, apart from that, two children died, so that family life became even more disagreeable for Ivan Ilyich.

In their new home Praskovya Feodorovna laid the blame for every mishap on her husband. Most of the subjects discussed by husband and wife, particularly the children's upbringing, led to questions that raised memories of former quarrels, and were always apt to raise fresh quarrels. There remained only those rare periods of love that overtook the couple but did not last long. They were islands at which they anchored briefly before setting sail once again over a sea of suppressed hostility, which was expressed in mutual aloofness. This aloofness could have saddened Ivan Ilyich had he thought it should not have been so, but by now he recognized that this situation was not only normal but the very aim of his role in the family. His aim increasingly was to free himself from these unpleasantnesses, to give them a character of harmless propriety, and he achieved this by spending less and less time with his family. When that was impossible, he tried to protect himself by having outsiders present. The main thing was that Ivan Ilyich had his work. All his interest in life was focused in his work. And this interest absorbed him. The consciousness of his own power, the potential to ruin anyone he wanted to ruin, the external pomp and real importance of his entry into court and his meetings with subordinates, his success in the eyes of high and low, and, above all, his mastery in conducting affairs, of which he was well aware—all this made him happy and, along with discussions with his friends, dinners and whist, filled his life. So that, all in all, Ivan Ilyich's life continued to pass as he thought it should: pleasantly and properly.

So he lived another seven years. His oldest daughter was already sixteen[15]; another child had died, and there remained his schoolboy son, the subject of dissension. Ivan Ilyich wanted to enter him in the School of Jurisprudence, but Praskovya Feodorovna sent him to high school, purely to spite him. His daughter was educated at home and was growing up well, and the boy was not doing badly either.

3

Ivan Ilyich's life continued in this way for seventeen years[16] after his marriage. He was by now a public prosecutor of long standing, having declined various transfers, waiting for a more desirable post, when, quite unexpectedly, something unpleasant happened, which nearly destroyed his peaceful life altogether. He was waiting for the post of presiding judge in a university town, but somehow Hoppe sneaked ahead and got the job. Ivan Ilyich lost his temper, complained, and quarreled with Hoppe and his immediate superiors. They grew distant toward him and in the next reshuffle he was passed over again.

This was in 1880. It was the worst year of Ivan Ilyich's life. In this year it became apparent that his salary was inadequate for his way of life, and, moreover, that everyone had forgotten him. What was more, the thing that seemed to be the most massive and grave injustice, as far as he was concerned, seemed to everyone else an ordinary matter. Even his father did not consider it his duty to help him. He felt that everyone had abandoned him, considering his position with an annual salary of 3,500 rubles quite normal, even fortunate. He alone knew that, what with his sense of how he had been slighted, the iniquities that had been done to him, his wife's endless nagging, and the debts he had started to build up, living as he did above his means—he alone knew that his position was far from normal.

In the summer of that year, to economize, he took leave and spent the summer months with his wife at his brother-in-law's place in the country.

In the country, without work, Ivan Ilyich experienced not only boredom but unbearable melancholy for the first time. He decided that living like this was impossible. It was essential to take some decisive action.

Having spent a sleepless night pacing the terrace, he made up his mind to travel to Petersburg and put pressure on the right people. He would transfer to a different ministry and punish the colleagues who failed to value him properly.

The next day he set off for Petersburg, in spite of his wife and brother-in-law's attempts to dissuade him.

He traveled with a single aim: to solicit a post that would bring him an annual salary of five thousand rubles. He was no longer set on any particular ministry, type, or area of work. All he needed was a post, any post bringing five thousand rubles—in government administration, in the banks, or the railways, or in the Empress Maria's institutions,[17] or even the customs—but the five thousand rubles were imperative, and it was imperative to leave the ministry where his merits went unrecognized.

And, lo and behold, this journey undertaken by Ivan Ilyich was crowned with extraordinary, unexpected success. At Kursk an acquaintance of his, F. S. Ilyin, joined him in his first-class carriage, and told him about a telegram received by the governor of Kursk with the white-hot news that in a few days there would be a shake-up in the ministry, and Piotr Ivanovich's place would be assigned to Ivan Simyonovich.

Apart from its importance for Russia, the predicted reshuffle[18] was particularly important for Ivan Ilyich, because it would bring into play a new figure, Piotr Petrovich, and, self-evidently, his friend Zakhar Ivanovich—and this was particularly favorable to Ivan Ilyich's own interests. Zakhar Ivanovich was an old friend and colleague of Ivan Ilyich.

The news was confirmed in Moscow. And when he reached Petersburg, Ivan Ilyich found Zakhar Ivanovich and was definitely promised a post in his old department, the Ministry of Justice.

A week later he telegraphed his wife: "Zakhar in Miller's place; my appointment follows first report."

Thanks to this change of personnel Ivan Ilyich unexpectedly obtained a grading in his previous ministry that set him two grades above his colleagues, with a salary of five thousand rubles, plus three thousand five hundred in removal allowances. All his resentment against his former enemies and the whole ministry was forgotten, and Ivan Ilyich was completely happy.

He returned to the country a cheerful and contented man, such as he had not been for a very long time. Praskovya Feodorovna also cheered up, and a truce was reached between them. Ivan Ilyich told how he was feted in Petersburg, how all those who had been his enemies had been put to shame and were fawning on him now, how everyone envied him for his new position, and, especially, he told them how everyone loved him in Petersburg.

Praskovya Feodorovna listened and pretended to believe it all, not contradicting him in anything, simply planning a new way of life in the town where they were going. And Ivan Ilyich saw with pleasure that her plans were his plans, that their interests coincided, and that his life, after a minor hiccup, was reverting to its due and proper character of cheerful pleasure and propriety.

Ivan Ilyich returned for only a short while. He had to take up his job on the tenth of September, and, besides, he needed time to settle into the new posting, move his belongings from the provinces, and in addition order and buy many new things—in a word, to set himself up in exactly the way he had himself decided, and almost exactly the same way as Praskovya Feodorovna had decided.

And now that everything was settled so well, he and his wife saw eye to eye. Apart from that, they spent little time together, and were more amiably inclined to each other than they had been since the first years of their married life. Ivan Ilyich thought he would take his family with him straight away, but the persuasions of his sister and her husband,[19] who had suddenly become particularly loving and familial toward him, resulted in his setting off alone.

Ivan Ilyich left, and the cheerful state of mind brought about by his success and the harmony with his wife, the one intensifying the other, continued to stay with him. An excellent set of apartments was found, exactly what both husband and wife had dreamed of. Spacious, high-ceilinged reception rooms in the old style, a comfortably imposing study, rooms for his wife and daughter, a schoolroom for his son—everything seemed made on purpose, just for them. Ivan Ilyich oversaw everything himself: he chose the wallpaper, bought more furniture, with a particular bent for old pieces, which he thought comme il faut, had them upholstered, and everything grew and grew, steadily approaching the ideal he set himself. When he had done only half of what he intended, the results far exceeded his expectations. He could already see that comme il faut elegance, that freedom from vulgarity everything would have when it was complete. Falling asleep, he imagined the reception room as it would become. Looking into the still-unfinished sitting room, he envisaged the fireplace, the fire screen, the étagère,[20] the occasional chairs, the dishes and plates displayed on the walls, the bronzes, when they would all be assembled in their place. The thought of how he would amaze Pasha and Lizanka,[21] who also had taste in these matters, made him glad. They can't possibly expect all this. Above all, he managed to find old furniture and buy it cheap, which gave everything a distinctly aristocratic flavor. In his letters he purposely described things worse than they were, in order to surprise them. It all absorbed him so much that his new job preoccupied him less than he expected, even though he liked that kind of work. When the court was in session he had moments of inattention; he would be pondering what kind of valances to have over the curtains, straight or curved. He was so taken up with it all that he often did things himself, moving the furniture and rehanging the curtains on his own. Once he climbed a small ladder to show the obtuse decorator how he wanted the fabric to be draped, missed his footing, and fell, but, being a strong and agile man, saved himself, only hitting his side against the handle of the window. The knock hurt for a little but soon passed off. Throughout this period Ivan Ilyich felt particularly well and cheerful. He wrote, "I feel as though fifteen years have simply slipped off me." He thought he would finish by September, but the work dragged on till mid-October. But then it looked delightful—not only he said so, but everyone who saw it said so to him.

In fact, however, the effect was the same as in the homes of all those people who are not quite rich enough, who want to look like the rich, and consequently look only like each other: damasks, mahogany, flowers, carpets and bronzes, dark woodstain and high polish—everything that people of a certain kind do to be like all other people of that certain kind. What he had was so similar to the norm that it did not even strike you, but to him everything seemed in some way extraordinary. When he met his family at the railway station and brought them to his completed, brightly lit apartments and a footman with a white tie opened the door to the flower-filled hall, and then they entered the reception room and the study, gasping with delight—he was very happy, leading them everywhere, drinking in their praise and beaming with pleasure. As they were taking tea the same evening, when Praskovya Feodorovna asked him, by the way, how did he come to fall, he laughed and showed them how he went flying and frightened the decorator.

"It's lucky I'm no mean gymnast. Another man would have killed himself, but I barely grazed myself, just here. It hurts when you touch it, but it's better already; it's just a bruise."

And they began living in their new home, where, as always, when you've settled in nicely, you find it's just one room too few; and living on their new income, which, as always, was just a tiny bit short—some five hundred rubles or so—and it was all very nice. The first period was particularly nice, when not everything had been done and there were still things to do: to buy one thing and order another, to shift this and adjust that. Although there were some differences of opinion between husband and wife, they were both so contented and there was so much to do that everything ended without major quarrels. When there was nothing left to arrange, it got a little boring and something seemed missing, but at this point they began acquiring new friends and habits and their life grew full.

Ivan Ilyich used to spend the mornings in court, returning home for dinner, and at first his humor was good, even though it was threatened precisely by his new home. (Every stain on the tablecloths and damasks, every broken blind cord irritated him: he had invested so much effort in getting things right that any flaw pained him.) But in general Ivan Ilyich's life continued in the way he thought his life should be—light, pleasant, and proper. He got up at nine, had some coffee, read the paper, then put on his uniform and drove off to the law courts. His working harness there had long been worn into shape and fitted him comfortably. Petitioners, office inquiries, the office itself, preliminary hearings in camera, public sessions. In all this one had to know how to exclude all the raw, living matter that invariably clogs the smooth running of official business. One had to guard against any relationship beyond the professional, the motive for human contact had to be exclusively professional and the contact itself had to remain exclusively professional. For instance, someone comes wanting some information. Not being officially responsible, Ivan Ilyich can have no contact with such a man—but if he has some official link with this person, something that can be identified on an officially headed sheet of paper, then, within the limits of this relationship Ivan Ilyich does everything, literally everything, that can be done, and moreover maintains a semblance of friendly human dealing— that is, of civility toward him. As soon as the official relationship is ended, so is everything else. Ivan Ilyich was a past master at this art of isolating his professional life, not allowing it to mix with his real life. With long practice and skill he had perfected it to such a degree that, like a virtuoso, he sometimes even allowed himself to mingle his private with his professional dealings—in jest, as it were. He allowed himself this because he felt he always had the power, when necessary, to fillet out the professional contact and jettison the human relationship. Ivan Ilyich managed this not merely lightly, pleasantly, and properly but with a virtuoso's skill. And in the idle intervals, he smoked, drank tea, discussed politics a little, general affairs a little, cards a little, and people's appointments most of all. And then, tired but with the feeling of a virtuoso who has duly played his part as one of the first violinists in the orchestra, he returned home. At home his daughter and wife had been out visiting somewhere or had been receiving visitors; his son had been to school and was doing his homework with his tutors, diligently learning the things that school makes one learn. Everything was well. After dinner, if there were no guests, Ivan Ilyich sometimes read a book that was in vogue, and in the evening sat down to work, that is, he read his papers, kept up with legislation, compared testimonies and sorted them under the appropriate laws. He found this neither dull nor engaging. It was dull when there was an opportunity to play cards, but if there were no card parties then it was at least better than sitting on his own or with his wife. Ivan Ilyich's pleasure lay in small dinner parties to which he invited socially prestigious men and women, passing the time with them in just the way that all such people pass their time, in a dining room that was just like all other dining rooms.

Once they even had a soirée and there was dancing. Ivan Ilyich enjoyed himself and everything went well, except that he had a big quarrel with his wife about the cakes and sweets: Praskovya Feodorovna had her own plans, but Ivan Ilyich insisted they should come from an expensive confectioner and ordered a lot of cakes and the quarrel was about the leftover cakes and the confectioner's bill, which came to forty-five rubles. It was a big quarrel and an unpleasant one, so much so that Praskovya Feodorovna called him "idiot, stupid moaner." And he tugged at his hair and angrily spoke of divorce. But the evening itself was very pleasant. The best people were there, and Ivan Ilyich danced with Princess Trufonov, the sister of the one well known for founding "Bear My Burden."[22] His professional pleasures were the pleasures of self-esteem, his social pleasures were the pleasures of vanity, but Ivan Ilyich's real pleasure was the pleasure of playing vint.[23] He used to admit that after everything, after whatever unpleasantnesses might have happened during his day, the one pleasure that shone like a candle, brighter than all others, was the prospect of sitting down with good players, poker-faced partners, to play vint, in a party of four of course (it's really unpleasant sitting out if there are five of you, even if you pretend oh, I love it), and to have an intelligent, serious game (when the cards are right), and then supper and a glass of wine. And after a game of vint, especially with small winnings (large ones were disagreeable), Ivan Ilyich went to bed in a particularly good humor.

So they lived. The very best people made up their circle, important people visited them, and young people, too.

Husband, wife, and daughter were entirely united about their circle and, without consulting each other, brushed off the ingratiating, shabbier friends and relatives that fluttered into their bright reception room hung with Japanese china. Soon the shabby friends stopped fluttering about and only the very best company remained at the Golovins. The young people paid court to Lizanka, and Petrishev, an examining magistrate, the son of Dmitri Ivanovich Petrishev and his only heir, began to pay such serious attention to her that Ivan Ilyich even began discussing it with Praskovya Feodorovna: should they not take them out for a troika ride or a trip to the theater? So they lived. And everything went on as usual and it was all very nice.

4

Everyone was well. You could hardly call it illness when Ivan Ilyich occasionally complained of a strange taste in his mouth and something that felt not quite right on the left side of his stomach.

But the mild discomfort began to increase, turning into something that was not yet quite a pain but an awareness of a permanent heaviness in his side and a poor state of mind. This poor state of mind grew stronger and stronger, beginning to spoil the light, pleasant, and proper way of life just established in the Golovin household. Husband and wife began quarreling more and more often, and soon the lightness and pleasantness of their life fell away and even propriety was barely maintained. Once again the arguments grew frequent. Once again only a few islands remained, and not many of those either, where husband and wife could still come to terms without an explosion.

And now Praskovya Feodorovna could say with some justification that her husband had a difficult character. With habitual exaggeration she maintained that he'd always had a horrible temper and she certainly needed her sweet nature to put up with it for twenty years. The truth was that now he started the quarrels. He always began carping just before dinner, often exactly when he started eating, during the soup course. He would notice a chipped dish, or something wrong with the food, or his son putting his elbows on the table, or his daughter's hairstyle. And he blamed Praskovya Feodorovna for everything. At first she objected and said unkind things back, but once or twice he became so enraged as dinner began, she realized it must be a constitutional disorder prompted by food and restrained herself, not answering back but only hurrying to get through the meal. Praskovya Feodorovna considered her self-restraint remarkably virtuous. Having decided her husband's appalling character made her life a misery, she grew sorry for herself. And the more she pitied herself, the more she loathed her husband. She started wishing he would die, but could not wish for that because then there would be no salary. And that made him even more irritating. She thought she was dreadfully unfortunate precisely because even his death could not save her. She was irritable, she concealed her irritation, and her hidden irritation aggravated his irritation.

After one scene when Ivan Ilyich was particularly unfair, he admitted in the subsequent explanations that he certainly was irritable but that was because of his illness. She told him that if he was ill then he should get treatment and insisted on his going to see an eminent doctor.

He went. Everything was as he expected; everything was done in the way it is always done. The waiting, and the pomp on entry, a charade played out by the doctor and familiar to him because it was the same as he recognized in himself in court, the tapping, and the listening, the questions requiring preordained and self-evidently futile replies, and the meaningful look which proclaimed, come, come sir, just rely on us and we'll sort it all out—we know perfectly well how to settle matters, one way will do for all, whoever they may be. It was all exactly as it was in court. Just as he put on a show in court for the man on trial, so the doctor put on a show for him.

The doctor said that such and such indicates that you have this and that inside, but if this isn't confirmed by the analysis of so-and-so and so-and-so, then we must assume you to have such and such and this and that. If, however, we assume so-and-so then... and so on. For Ivan Ilyich only one question was important: was his condition dangerous or not? But the doctor ignored this irrelevant question. From the doctor's point of view it was an idle speculation not requiring resolution: the only thing was to weigh up the probabilities of a floating kidney, chronic catarrh, or a disease of the blind gut.[24] It was not Ivan Ilyich's life that was in question, but the rival merits of the floating kidney and blind gut. And under Ivan Ilyich's eyes the doctor brilliantly found in favor of the floating kidney, with the one reservation that the investigation of the urine might provide new evidence, which would justify reassessment. All this was exactly what Ivan Ilyich had done himself a thousand times, dealing with defendants in this dazzling manner. The doctor made his summing-up just as brilliantly, looking over his spectacles triumphantly and even gaily at the accused. From the doctor's summing-up Ivan Ilyich drew the conclusion that things were bad. For the doctor and quite probably for everyone, it didn't matter a damn, but for him it was bad. And this conclusion struck Ivan Ilyich painfully, arousing in him a feeling of intense pity for himself and great bitterness against the doctor, who was so indifferent to a question of such importance.

But he said nothing, stood up, put his money on the desk, and said with a sigh, "I imagine we sick people often ask you irrelevant questions.... By and large, is it a dangerous illness or not?"

With one eye the doctor looked at him sternly through his spectacles, as though to say: prisoner in the dock, if you do not confine yourself to the questions put to you, I will be obliged to require your removal from the court.

"I have already told you what I deem necessary and appropriate," said the doctor. "Further evidence will come from the analysis." And the doctor bowed.

Ivan Ilyich went out slowly, drearily took his place in the sleigh, and drove home. For the entire journey he went over everything the doctor had said, incessantly trying to translate all those tangled, obscure technical terms into plain language and to decipher from them the answer to his question: it is bad—but is it very bad for me or not so bad yet? And it seemed to him that the implication of everything the doctor had said was that it was very bad. Everything in the streets seemed sad to Ivan Ilyich. The coachmen were sad, the houses were sad, the passersby and the shops were sad. And that dull, gnawing pain that never eased seemed to take on a different, more serious significance from the doctor's obscure pronouncements. Ivan Ilyich attended to it with a new feeling of heaviness.

He drove home to tell his wife. She was going to hear him out, but in the middle of his account his daughter came in with her hat on: she was about to go out with her mother. With an effort she sat down to listen to this tedious stuff, could not contain herself for long, and her mother stopped listening.

"Well, I'm delighted," said Praskovya Feodorovna. "Now mind you take the medicine properly. Give me the prescription and I'll send Gerasim to the chemist." And she went to put her coat on.

He had not paused for breath while she was in the room, and sighed heavily when she left.

"Well, who knows," he said. "Maybe it really is nothing much."

He began taking the medicines and followed the doctor's directions, which changed after the urine analysis. But then, immediately, there was some sort of muddle over the analysis and consequent instructions. The doctor could not be reached, and it turned out that Ivan Ilyich was not doing what the doctor had ordered. Either the doctor had forgotten something, or lied about something, or concealed something from him.

Nevertheless, Ivan Ilyich began following the instructions meticulously, and even found some comfort in this at first.

After the visit to the doctor Ivan Ilyich's main occupation became the precise fulfillment of his recommendations about hygiene, taking his medicine, and the attentive observation of his pain and all his bodily functions. His chief interests were people's ailments and people's health. When others spoke in his presence about sicknesses, deaths, recoveries, and particularly about illnesses similar to his own, he tried to hide his anxiety, listening intently, questioning closely, and finding similarities to his own condition.

The pain grew no less, but Ivan Ilyich made great efforts forcibly to persuade himself that he felt better. And he was able to deceive himself so long as nothing upset him. But as soon as there was a disagreement with his wife, or something went wrong at work, or he had a bad hand at cards, he promptly felt the full force of the disease. In the past he met failure with sanguine expectation—I can put it right in a trice, I'll get the better of him, I'll wait for success, for a grand slam. But now with every failure he lost heart and despaired. He said to himself, "I was just getting better; the medicine was finally beginning to work—and now this dratted misfortune, this damned unpleasantness...." And he raged against the mishap, or the people responsible for it who were killing him, and he could feel his own anger killing him but was unable to restrain himself. You might think he should have realized that his fury against people and circumstances aggravated his illness and consequently he should avoid paying attention to any unpleasantnesses, but his reasoning went the opposite way—he said he needed peace of mind, scrutinized everything that might disrupt his peace of mind, and the slightest disruption infuriated him. His situation was exacerbated by reading medical textbooks and seeking advice from doctors. The deterioration continued so smoothly he was able to deceive himself when he compared one day to the next—there was little difference. But when he asked for medical advice it seemed to him that everything was getting worse, and very quickly, too. And yet he continued to consult the doctors, regardless.

That month he went to another eminent specialist, and that eminence said almost the same as the first one but posed the questions slightly differently. The advice of this eminence only intensified Ivan Ilyich's doubts and fears. A friend of a friend—a very good doctor—

diagnosed his illness completely differently, and even though he promised recovery, his questions and hypotheses further confused Ivan Ilyich and confirmed his doubts. A homeopath identified his illness in yet another way and gave him some medicine, which Ivan Ilyich took in secret for a week. But when he felt no improvement after a week he lost faith in that cure and all the others, and fell into even profounder gloom. On one occasion a lady of his acquaintance told him about healing icons. Ivan Ilyich caught himself listening attentively and crediting her facts. This episode frightened him. "Can I really have gone so weak in the head?" he thought. "What rubbish! It's all nonsense. I mustn't give in to hypochondria. I must choose one doctor and keep strictly to his course of treatment. That's what I'll do. There's an end of it. I'll stop thinking and stick strictly to one cure till the summer. And then we'll see. Enough of this dithering." It was easy to say, and impossible to do. The pain in his side kept wearing him down and seemed to be getting steadily more sustained and severe. The taste in his mouth grew more and more peculiar; it felt to him as though some revolting smell was coming out of his mouth, and his strength and appetite were both diminishing. He could not deceive himself: something terrifying, new, and incomparably significant—more significant than anything in Ivan Ilyich's previous life—was taking place inside him. And he was the only one who knew about it. Everyone around him did not understand, or did not want to understand, and thought that everything in the world was going on as usual. This was what tormented Ivan Ilyich more than anything. The people at home—principally his wife and daughter, who were caught up in a positive whirl of visits—understood nothing, as he could see, and were irritated by how demanding and cheerless he was, as though this were his fault. Even though they tried to disguise it, he could see that he was a hindrance to them, but that his wife had worked out a definite response to his illness and stuck to it in spite of anything he might say or do. Her approach went like this: "You know," she would say to their acquaintances, "Ivan Ilyich can't follow a course of treatment strictly, like any other self-respecting person. One day he takes the drops and eats what he's ordered, and goes to bed in good time, and the next day, if I don't keep an eye on him, he forgets to take anything, eats sturgeon (which is against the doctor's orders), and, what's more, stays up for a game of vint till one in the morning."

"Oh come, when was that?" Ivan Ilyich says in vexation. "Only once, at Piotr Ivanovich's."

"And yesterday at Shebek's."

"What difference did that make? I couldn't sleep for pain."

"What nonsense. Whatever you say, you'll never get well like this—you'll just go on making us miserable."

Praskovya Feodorovna's attitude to her husband's illness, which she expressed quite openly to others and himself, was that Ivan Ilyich was to blame for his illness and the whole illness was a new unpleasantness he was inflicting on his wife. Ivan Ilyich felt that she let this slip involuntarily, but it made matters no easier for him.

At court Ivan Ilyich also noticed, or thought he noticed, the same curious attitude toward him. Sometimes he thought people were eyeing him like a man soon to vacate his post, and then his friends would suddenly start teasing him for being morbid—as though that terrible, terrifying, unheard-of thing infesting him from within, incessantly sucking away at him and irresistibly dragging him off somewhere, were the most delightful topic for a joke. He was particularly irritated by Schwartz's lively, comme-il-faut playfulness, which reminded Ivan Ilyich of himself ten years ago.

His friends would come over for a game of cards, and sit down. The new packs were fanned, shuffled, and dealt; Ivan Ilyich sorted his hand into suits. Seven diamonds. His partner said, "No trumps," and led with the two of diamonds. What more could he want? Delightful, capital it should have been—they would make a grand slam. And suddenly Ivan Ilyich feels that pain sucking away at him, that taste in his mouth, and it seems grotesque to him that in the midst of this he could feel pleased by a grand slam.

He steals a glance at his partner, Mikhail Mikhailovich, who raps the tabletop with an energetic hand and courteously, indulgently restrains himself from snatching up the tricks, moving them across to Ivan Ilyich instead, giving him the pleasure of collecting them without incommoding himself, barely stretching out his hand. "What does he think I am, so feeble I can't even stretch my hand out?" thinks Ivan Ilyich. And he forgets the trumps,[25] trumps his partner's winning card, misses the grand slam by three tricks, and—which is worse than everything—sees how upset Mikhail Mikhailovich is, while he doesn't care. And it is dreadful to think what it is that makes him not care.

Everyone sees it is difficult for him, and they say, "Why don't we stop, if you're tired? Have a rest." A rest? No, no, he's not in the least tired; they must finish the rubber. Everyone is silent and gloomy. Ivan Ilyich feels as though he has let this misery loose on them and can't dispel it. They dine together and go their ways, and Ivan Ilyich is left alone in the knowledge that his life is poisoned and poisons the lives of others and that this poison does not diminish, but permeates his whole existence more and more profoundly.

With this knowledge, and with his physical pain, and with his terror beyond that, he had to go to bed and often lie most of the night sleepless from pain. And then in the morning he had to get up again, get dressed, drive off to court, speak and write, or, if he did not go to work, he had to sit out those twenty-four hours of every day at home, of which every minute was a torment. And he had to live in this way, on the very edge of destruction, without a single being who might understand and pity him.

5

So one month passed, and another. Just before the new year his brother-in-law came to town to stay with them. Ivan Ilyich was in court. Praskovya Feodorovna was out shopping. When Ivan Ilyich returned, he found his brother-in-law, a healthy, ruddy-faced man, unpacking his case in Ivan Ilyich's study. Hearing Ivan Ilyich's footsteps, he lifted his head and glanced at him in silence for a few moments. For Ivan Ilyich that look made everything clear. His brother-in-law opened his mouth to gasp, and just stopped himself. That movement confirmed it all.

"What, have I changed?"

"Yes...there is a change."

And however hard Ivan Ilyich tried to turn the conversation to his appearance, his brother-in-law said nothing. Praskovya Feodorovna returned home, and her brother went to her quarters. Ivan Ilyich locked his study door and started scrutinizing himself in the mirror—full face first, then from the side. He picked up the portrait photograph of himself with his wife and compared it with what he saw in the glass. The change was enormous. Then he bared his arms to the elbow, looked at them, rolled down his sleeves, sat down on the ottoman, and grew black as night.

"No, no; I mustn't," he said to himself, jumped up, went to his desk, took out his papers, and started reading them, but could not. He unlocked his door and went out into the hall. The door to the sitting room was shut. He tiptoed up to it and started listening.

"Nonsense, you're exaggerating," Praskovya Feodorovna was saying.

"What do you mean, exaggerating? You can't see it—he's a dead man, look at his eyes. There's no light in them. What's wrong with him, anyway?"

"No one knows. Nikolayev"—that was another doctor—"said something, but I don't know. Leschititsky"—that was the famous doctor—"said the opposite. . . ."

Ivan Ilyich withdrew, went into his study, lay down, and began thinking "the kidney, the floating kidney." He remembered everything the doctors had told him, how the kidney had torn loose and was floating about. And with all the force of his imagination he tried to catch his kidney, pin it down, and stop it wandering. So little was needed, it seemed to him. "No; I'll go back to Piotr Ivanovich." (That was the friend who had a doctor friend.) He rang, ordered the horse to be harnessed to the sleigh, and prepared to leave.

"Where are you going, Jean[26]?" his wife asked, with a particularly sad and uncharacteristically kind expression.

Her uncharacteristic gentleness riled him. He looked at her sourly.

"I have to go to Piotr Ivanovich."

He drove off to his friend who had the friend who was a doctor. And with him he drove to the doctor. He found him in and had a long talk with him.

Reviewing the anatomical and physiological details of what the doctor thought was going on inside him, Ivan Ilyich understood it all.

There was some little thing, a minute little something, in the blind gut. It could all get better. It was just a matter of increasing the energy of one organ and diminishing the activity of another; absorption would take place and everything would get better. He was a little late for dinner, ate and talked cheerfully, but for a long time could not go to his room to work. Finally he went into his study and promptly sat down to his files. He read them, worked at them, but the consciousness that he had postponed an important, intimate business he would deal with as soon as he finished, did not leave him. When he finished his papers, he remembered that this intimate business was to think about his blind gut. But he did not succumb; he went into the drawing room for tea. There were guests; people were talking and playing the piano; there was singing; the examining magistrate, the desirable match for his daughter, was there. Praskovya Feodorovna observed that Ivan Ilyich spent the evening more cheerfully than anyone, but he did not forget for a minute that he had laid aside important thoughts about his blind gut. At eleven o'clock he excused himself and went to his quarters. Since the beginning of his illness he had been sleeping alone in a small room off his study. He entered, undressed, took up a novel by Zola, but instead of reading it he thought. And in his imagination the desired correction of his blind gut came about. Absorption was taking place; evacuation occurred, correct functioning was reestablished. "Yes, that's how it should be," he thought; "we just have to give nature a hand." He remembered his medicine, sat up, took it, lay on his back, and attended to how the medicine was putting things right and diminishing his pain. "I just have to take it steadily and avoid adverse influences; even now I feel a little better—a lot better." He began pinching his side and it did not hurt from the pinch. "Yes, I can't feel it; it really is a lot better already." He blew out his candle and lay on his side. The blind gut was setting itself right; it was becoming absorbed. Suddenly he felt the familiar old, dull, gnawing pain, stubborn, quiet, and grave. The familiar disgusting stuff in his mouth. His heart contracted, his head clouded. "My God! My God!" he said. "Again, and again, and it will never end." And suddenly the whole thing appeared to him in a different light. "Blind gut! Kidney!" he said to himself. "It's not a matter of the blind gut or the kidney but of life and . . . death. Yes, there was life and now it's going, it's going, and I can't hold it back. Yes. Why should I deceive myself? Isn't it obvious to everyone except me that I'm dying, and it's only a question of how many weeks, days—even now, maybe. There was light, and now it's dark. I was here, and now I'm going there! Where?" A chill ran through him; his breathing stopped. He could hear only the beating of his heart.

"I'll be no more, and then what will there be? Nothing. Then where will I be, when I will be no longer? Is this really death? Go away, I don't want you." He sat upright, wanting to light his candle, fumbled with trembling hands, dropped candle and candlestick on the floor, and fell back on his pillow. "What for? It doesn't make any difference," he said to himself, staring with open eyes into the dark. "Death. Yes, death. And none of them know, and none of them want to know, and none of them are sorry. They're having fun." (From beyond his door he heard the distant sound of voices and a musical ritornello.) "They don't care, but they'll die just like me. Idiocy. Sooner for me, later for them, but it will come. And they're happy. Mindless brutes!" He was choked with resentment. And he grew agonizingly, unbearably sick at heart. It cannot be that everyone, always, is doomed to this awful horror. He sat up.

"Something's wrong. I must calm down and think everything through from the beginning." And he started thinking it out. "Yes, there was the beginning of the illness. I knocked my side, but was the same before and after; it ached a bit, and then a bit more, and then there were doctors, and then depression, dreariness, doctors again, and I kept coming closer and closer to the abyss. Less strength. Closer and closer. And here I am, wasted away, no light in my eyes. This is death, and I'm thinking about my gut. I'm thinking about putting my kidney right, and this is death. Can this really be death?" Panic overcame him again, he lost his breath, bent over to look for matches, and knocked his elbow on the bedside table. The table got in his way and hurt him; he lost his temper, pushed it harder in his vexation, and knocked it over. And, in despair, barely able to breathe, he fell back expecting instant death.

At this time the guests were taking their leave. Praskovya Feodorovna was seeing them out. She heard something fall and came in.

"What's the matter?"

"Nothing. I dropped it, by accident."

She went out and came back with a candle. He lay there, breathing fast and hard, like a man who has run a mile, looking at her with a fixed stare.

"What is it, Jean?"

"N—nothing. I...dro—dropped it...." (Why bother to say? She won't understand, he thought.)

Certainly she did not understand. She picked up his candle, lit it, and left hastily; there was a last guest to see to.

When she returned, he was still lying on his back, staring above him.

"What is it; are you worse?"

"Yes."

She shook her head and sat by him awhile.

"You know, Jean, I'm wondering whether we should get Leschititsky to visit you here."

That meant calling out the famous doctor without a thought for the expense. He smiled poisonously and said, "No." She sat a little longer, went up to him, and kissed him on the forehead.

At that moment, as she kissed him, he hated her with all the strength of his soul and had to make an effort not to push her away.

"Good night. God willing, you'll fall asleep."

"Yes."

6

Ivan Ilyich saw that he was dying, and was in continual despair.

In the depths of his soul Ivan Ilyich knew that he was dying, but he could not get used to the idea, and, more than that, he simply did not and could not take it in.

All his life the example of a syllogism he had learned in Kiesewetter's logic[27]—Caius is a man; men are mortal; therefore Caius is mortal—seemed to him to be correct only in relation to Caius and in no way to himself. There was Caius the man, man in general, and that was quite fair—but he was not Caius and not man in general. He was always quite,

quite different from all other beings. He was little Vanya with Mamma, with Papa, with Mitya and Volodya and his toys and the coachman and his nanny and then with Katenka[28], with all the joys and sorrows and passions of childhood, youth, and adolescence. Did Caius know the smell of the striped leather ball Vanya loved so much? Did Caius kiss his mother's hand like him, and did the silk pleats of his mother's dress rustle like that for Caius? Did Caius clamor for pasties at school? Did Caius ever fall in love like him? Could Caius chair a session like him?

Naturally Caius was mortal, and it was right for him to die, but for me, Vanya, Ivan Ilyich, with all my feelings and thoughts—for me it is another matter. And it cannot be right for me to die. That would be too terrible.

That was what he felt.

"If I also had to die, like Caius, then I would have known it, my inner voice would have told me so. But there was nothing of the sort inside me. Both I and all my friends—we understood that for us it was nothing like it was for Caius. And now look!" he said to himself. "It can't be. It can't be, but it is. How can it be? How can I understand it?"

He could not comprehend it, and tried to drive the thought away as something mendacious, mistaken, morbid, crowding it out with different, acceptable, and healthy thoughts. But the thought was not only a thought, it was like a reality that returned to stand before him.

And he called up other thoughts in turn to take the place of this thought, hoping to find support from them. He tried to return to his old habits of mind, which had screened him in the past from the thought of death. But, strange to say, everything that had screened him in the past, obscuring and abolishing the awareness of death, could not do so any longer. In these days Ivan Ilyich spent most of his time trying to reestablish the old train of thoughts that had once screened him from death. Sometimes he said to himself, "I'll get back to work; after all, that was my life." And he went to court, shaking off any doubts; he chatted with his friends and took his place as he always had done, a trifle absentmindedly, casting a thoughtful glance over the crowd and, bracing himself with both emaciated hands on the arms of his chair, inclined his head as usual to his colleague, moving matters along in a whisper—and then, abruptly raising his eyes and seating himself straight, pronounced the familiar words that opened the proceedings. But suddenly the pain in his side, not paying the least attention to the stage reached in the hearing, started *its* business, sucking away at him. Ivan Ilyich listened to the proceedings, beating off the thought of it but it held its own. *It* came up and stood right in front of him, and looked at him, and he froze, the light died out of his eyes, and once more he started asking himself, "Surely *it* can't be the only truth?" And his colleagues and subordinates watched with regret and surprise as he, such an acute and dazzling judge, got confused and made mistakes. He would shake himself, trying to collect his thoughts and carry the proceedings to a conclusion somehow or other. He drove home in the sad knowledge that his court duties could no longer conceal from him the thing he wanted to conceal—his court duties could not free him from *it*. And what was worst of all was that *it* drew his attention to itself, not for him to do something different, but only for him to look *it* straight in the eyes, look at *it* and, having nothing else to do, suffer unspeakably.

To save himself from this situation, Ivan Ilyich searched for other consolations, other screens—and other screens were found and for a short time seemed to save him. But soon enough they did not quite fall to pieces so much as wear thin, as though *it* penetrated everything, and nothing could shield him from *its* glare.

In these days he went into the drawing room that he had furnished—the drawing room where he fell, and for whose décor (so the venomous absurdity of it struck him) he had sacrificed his life. He knew his illness began with that bruise. Coming into the drawing room he noticed that the lacquered table had been scratched by something and, searching for a cause, found it in the album with the brass openwork cover that was twisted at one corner. He picked up the album, a costly one he had lovingly arranged himself, vexed by the thoughtlessness of his daughter and her friends—one picture torn, others in disarray—and painstakingly put it in order, bending back the brass corner.

Then it occurred to him to move the whole *établissement*[29] with the photograph albums into a different corner where the flowers stood. He called the footman; either his wife or daughter came to help, they disagreed and contradicted each other; he argued and grew cross; but everything was all right, because he was not remembering *it*—*it* could not be seen.

But then, as he was moving everything himself, his wife happened to say, "Leave it, the servants can do that; you'll only do yourself another injury," and suddenly *it* flickered through the screen, he caught sight of *it*. It was only a glimpse; he still hoped *it* would withdraw from view, but involuntarily he attended to his side—and there it is, the same thing still crouching there, gnawing away. He can no longer forget anything, and *it* is distinctly staring at him from behind the flowers. What is the point of it all?

"And it's true that I lost my life climbing up to this curtain, like a man on the barricades. Can that really be true? How terrible and how stupid! It can't be! It can't be, and it is."

He went back to his study to lie down. He was alone with *it* again. Face-to-face with *it*, and nothing to do. Just look at *it* and grow cold.

7

How it came about would be impossible to say, because it happened imperceptibly, inch by inch, but in the third month of Ivan Ilyich's illness it came to pass that both his wife, his daughter, his son, the servants, and friends, and doctors, and, above all he himself all knew that their only interest in him lay in how quickly he would vacate his post at last, free the living from the constraints imposed by his presence, and himself be freed from suffering.

He slept less and less; he was given opium and injections of morphine. But it made things no easier for him. The dull misery he felt in his semisoporific state at first relieved him only by being something new; but afterward it became as harrowing as frank pain, or even worse.

They prepared special food for him in accordance with the doctors' instructions, but the dishes grew more and more tasteless and disgusting to him.

Special arrangements were also made for his excretions, and he found them unbearable every time. He was tormented by the dirt, the indecency, the smell, and the knowledge that another person had to take part.

But in this most unpleasant business Ivan Ilyich's consolation came to light. It was Gerasim, the peasant who served at table, who always came to carry out the soil.

Gerasim was a clean, fresh young peasant who had thrived on city food. He was always bright and cheerful. At first the sight of this lad, always cleanly dressed in the Russian style, doing this disgusting work, discomfited Ivan Ilyich. Once he got up from the commode and was unable to pull up his trousers. He fell into a padded armchair and looked in horror at his powerless naked thighs with their starkly marked muscles.

Gerasim entered with his light, strong step in his thick boots, bringing with him a pleasant smell of tar from his boots and fresh winter air. Wearing a clean homespun apron and clean cotton-print rubakha,[30] his sleeves rolled up his strong, bare young arms, and not looking at Ivan Ilyich—evidently withholding his pleasure in life that shone in his face, so as not to offend the sick man—he went up to the commode.

"Gerasim," said Ivan Ilyich weakly.

Gerasim started, evidently alarmed that he might have done something wrong, and with a quick movement turned to the invalid his fresh, kind, simple young face that was just beginning to show signs of a beard.

"Can I do anything for you?"

"I think that must be unpleasant for you. You must forgive me. I can't help it."

"Not at all, sir." And Gerasim beamed with white young teeth and bright eyes. "Why shouldn't I take a little trouble? You're not so well."

And with deft, strong hands he did his usual task and went out on light feet. And five minutes later returned stepping as lightly as before.

Ivan Ilyich had not moved from the armchair.

"Gerasim," he said, when the lad had replaced the clean pan. "Could you help me please? Just come over here." Gerasim came up. "Lift me up. It's hard for me on my own, but I told Dmitri he could go."

Gerasim came right up to him; put his strong arms around him; and with the lightness of his step, deftly, gently lifted him up and steadied him, pulling up his trousers with the other hand. He was about to sit him down again, but Ivan Ilyich asked him to take him to the divan. Effortlessly and without apparent pressure, Gerasim led him, almost carrying him, to the divan and settled him down.

"Thank you. How lightly, how well … you do everything."

Gerasim smiled again and wanted to leave. But it felt so good to be with him that Ivan Ilyich did not want to let him go.

"I tell you what; move up that chair for me, please. No, that one, under my legs. It's easier for me when my feet are raised."

Gerasim carried the chair across, set it down steadily without knocking it, and lifted Ivan Ilyich's legs onto the chair. It seemed to Ivan Ilyich that he felt better while Gerasim was lifting his legs up.

"I feel better when my legs are high," said Ivan Ilyich. "Put that cushion over there under them."

Gerasim did so. Once more he lifted up his legs and put them down again. Once more Ivan Ilyich felt eased while Gerasim was holding up his legs. When he laid them down he seemed to feel worse again.

"Gerasim," he said to him, "are you busy at the moment?"

"Not in the least, your honor," said Gerasim, who had learned from the city folk how to speak to the gentry.

"What have you still got to do?"

"What, me? I've nothing to do, I've done it all—there's only the wood to chop for tomorrow."

"Then hold my legs up like that a bit, could you?"

"Of course I can." And Gerasim lifted up his legs, and it appeared to Ivan Ilyich that in that position he felt no pain at all.

"But what about the firewood?"

"Don't you worry about that, sir. We'll find time."

Ivan Ilyich told Gerasim to sit down and hold his legs, and talked to him. And, strange to say, it seemed to him that he felt better while Gerasim was holding up his legs.

From that time Ivan Ilyich began calling for Gerasim occasionally. He would make him hold his legs up on his shoulders, and liked talking to him. Gerasim did so lightly, willingly, with a simplicity and kindness that touched Ivan Ilyich. He was offended by health, strength, and good spirits in everyone else, but Gerasim's strength and cheerfulness soothed him rather than hurting him.

Ivan Ilyich suffered most of all from lies—the lie that everyone accepted, for some reason, that he was just ill, not dying, that he need only keep calm and take his medicine and something splendid would come of it. And he knew that whatever the medicines might do, nothing would come of it except more agonizing misery and death. He found this lie insufferable; he was tormented by the fact that nobody wanted to admit what he knew—what everyone knew—but chose to lie to him about his dreadful state. They wanted, even forced him to participate in the same lie. Lying—the lie inflicted on him on the eve of his death, the lie which was bound to degrade the fearful, solemn scene of his death to the level of all those visits, curtains, and sturgeons for dinner...this was a dreadful affliction for Ivan Ilyich. And—it was strange—many times when they were doing their stuff over him, he was within a whisker of shouting at them, "Stop lying! You know and I know I'm dying, at least you could stop lying to me." But he never had the spirit to do so. He could see that the terrifying, awesome act of his dying was reduced by everyone around him to the level of a casual unpleasantness, to some extent an offense against propriety (rather in the way people behave to someone who brings a bad smell into the room with him). And *this* was the propriety he had served all his life. He saw that no one would pity him, because no one even wanted to understand his position. Only Gerasim understood his situation and was sorry for him. It was good for him when Gerasim held his legs on his shoulders, sometimes for whole nights at a stretch, and did not want to go to bed, saying, "You mustn't worry, Ivan Ilyich, I'll get my sleep another time," or when he once slipped into the intimate form of address, saying, "With thee so poorly, how couldn't I spare a little trouble?" Gerasim alone did not lie to him; it was obvious from everything that he alone understood what was happening, saw no need to hide it, and was simply sorry for his weak and wasted master. Once he even said so straight out, when Ivan Ilyich was sending him away: "We'll all go someday. Why not take a little trouble?" he said, expressing in this way that he did not grudge his pains precisely because they were taken for a dying man and he hoped that in his own time someone else would take the same pains for him.

Apart from this lie, or as a result of it, the most painful thing for Ivan Ilyich was that no one pitied him as he wanted to be pitied. At certain moments after long-drawn-out pain, he wanted most of all (ashamed though he would have been to admit it)—he wanted someone to pity him as a sick child is pitied. He wanted them to stroke him, kiss him, cry a little over him, as children are cuddled and consoled. He knew he was an important member of the court, that his beard was going gray, and so it had to be out of the question, but it was still what he wanted. In his relationship with Gerasim there was something close to this, and consequently his relationship with Gerasim comforted him. Ivan Ilyich wants to cry, he wants to be stroked, to have them crying over him—and in comes his friend, court member Shebek, and instead of tears and tenderness Ivan Ilyich puts on a serious, stern expression, a face full of profound thought, and through sheer inertia pronounces his opinion on the implications of the decision taken by the Court of Appeal, and stubbornly insists on his view. More than anything, this lie around him and in himself poisoned the last days of Ivan Ilyich's life.

8

It was morning. It was only morning because Gerasim left and Piotr the footman came in, blew out the candles, drew one curtain, and started quietly tidying up. Morning or evening, Friday or Sunday—it made no difference, it was all one, always the same. Gnawing, agonizing pain, not slackening for a second; the consciousness of life passing hopelessly but still not past; death moving up on him, terrifying, hateful, changeless death which was the one reality, and all the old lies. What were days, weeks, and hours of day to him?

"Would you care to order tea?"

Piotr wants tidy routines, and so the gentry must take their tea in the mornings, Ivan Ilyich thought, and answered only "No."

"Would you wish to move to the divan?"

He needs to put the room straight and I'm in the way; I'm dirt and disorder, he thought, and said only, "No, leave me."

The footman busied himself awhile. Ivan Ilyich stretched his hand out. The footman came up obsequiously.

"Would you require something, sir?"

"My watch."

Piotr picked up the watch just by Ivan Ilyich's hand, and gave it to him.

"Half past eight. Are the others up?"

"No, your honor. Vassili Ivanovich" (that was his son) "has gone to school. Praskovya Feodorovna gave orders to be woken if you asked for her. Would you require it?"[31]

"No, there's no need." Should I try some tea? he thought. "Yes, tea . . . you could bring it."

Piotr went to the door. Ivan Ilyich grew frightened of being left on his own. How can I stop him? Ah yes, the medicine. "Piotr, give me my medicine." You never know, maybe the medicine might still help. He took the spoonful and swallowed it. No, it won't help, that's all rubbish and lies, he decided, as soon as he encountered the familiar, sickly, hopeless taste. No, I can't believe in it anymore. But that pain, that pain, I wish it would ease even just for a minute. And he groaned. Piotr came back. "No, go. Bring me the tea."

Piotr went out. Left on his own, Ivan Ilyich groaned, not so much from pain, however dreadful it was, as from misery. They're all the same, all these endless nights and days. Would that it came quicker. What should come quicker? Death, darkness? No, no. Everything is better than death!

When Piotr came in with the tea tray, Ivan Ilyich stared dazedly at him for a long time, not understanding who he was and why. Piotr was embarrassed by his stare, and his embarrassment brought Ivan Ilyich back to himself.

"Ah yes, the tea," he said. "Very well, put it down. Only help me wash and change my shirt."

And Ivan Ilyich began washing. With pauses for rest he washed his hands, his face, he brushed his teeth, he started brushing his hair and glanced in the mirror. He became frightened; what was most frightening was the way his hair clung flat to his pallid forehead.

When they were changing his shirt, he knew it would be even more frightening to look down at his body, and he did not look at himself. But now everything was done. He put on his dressing gown, covered himself with a plaid rug, and sat down to his tea in the armchair. For a minute he felt refreshed, but as soon as he started drinking his tea, there was the same foul taste and pain again. With an effort he finished the tea and lay down, his legs outstretched. He lay back and dismissed Piotr.

Everything always the same. Then hope glints—like a drop of water. A drop lost in a turbulent ocean of despair. And everything is pain again, pain and misery and everything always the same. It is dreadfully sad on his own; he longs to call somebody but knows in advance that it is even worse with others there. "If only I could have some morphine, I might lose consciousness. I'll tell him, that doctor, he must think of something else. It's impossible, impossible to go on like this."

In this way one hour passes, and another. But now the bell rings in the hall. Maybe it's the doctor. Exactly so: it is the doctor—fresh, brisk, fat, and cheerful, with that expression that says—there you are, all in a panic for some reason, but in a minute we'll put everything right. The doctor knows his expression is inappropriate here, but he has put it on once and for all and cannot take it off again, like a man who has put on tails in the morning and driven off to pay a round of calls with no opportunity to change.

The doctor rubs his hands briskly, comfortingly.

"My hands are chilly. It's quite a frost. Let me just get warm," he says, with that expression, as though they only need wait a little till he gets warm, and once he's warm he'll put everything right.

"Well now, how—"

Ivan Ilyich feels the doctor wanted to say, "How's tricks?" but realizes one cannot talk like that, and says instead, "How did you pass the night?"

Ivan Ilyich looks at the doctor with an expression that asks, Will you never feel ashamed of your lies? But the doctor does not want to understand his question.

And Ivan Ilyich says, "It's all so dreadful. The pain won't stop, not even ease for a little. If only there was something!"

"Yes, you sick men always say that. Well, now, I think I've got a little warmer, even Praskovya Feodorovna, such a stickler for correctness, couldn't find fault with my temperature. Well, now, how do you do?" And the doctor shakes his hand.

And, dropping all his former jocularity, with a serious expression, the doctor starts examining his patient's pulse and temperature, and the tapping and listening begins.

Ivan Ilyich knows definitely and indubitably that this is all nonsense, a hollow sham, but when the doctor gets down on his knees, stretches over him, pressing his ear now higher, now lower, going through a variety of gymnastic arabesques over his body with the most significant expression, Ivan Ilyich allows himself to be taken in, as in the old days he gave in to the lawyers' speeches when he knew perfectly well that they were all lying and why they were lying.

The doctor was kneeling on the divan, still tapping away at something, when Praskovya Feodorovna's silk dress rustled at the door, and her voice was heard rebuking Piotr for failing to announce the doctor's arrival.

She comes in, kisses her husband, and immediately begins proving she was up long ago. She was only absent when the doctor arrived because of a misunderstanding.

Ivan Ilyich looks at her, scrutinizes her all over, and takes exception to her plump, white, clean hands and neck, her shiny hair and bright eyes, full of life. He detests her with all the strength of his soul. And her touch makes him suffer from his surge of hatred.

Her attitude to him and his illness is still the same. Just as the doctor has worked out an attitude to his patients which he can no longer shake off, so she has worked out her attitude to him—that he isn't doing something he ought to be doing, and it's all his fault, while she lovingly reproaches him—and is now quite unable to divest herself of this attitude.

"He just won't do as he's told! He *will* not take the drops on time. But the main thing is, he lies down in a position that must surely be bad for him, with his legs in the air."

She tells how he makes Gerasim hold up his legs.

The doctor smiles gently-derisively. What are we to do? These invalids sometimes think up the funniest things, but we can forgive them.

When the examination was over the doctor looked at his watch, and only then did Praskovya Feodorovna announce that whether Ivan Ilyich liked it or not, she had invited the distinguished doctor to come today, to examine him and discuss his condition with Mikhail Danilovich (as the ordinary doctor was called).

"Please don't protest. I'm doing it entirely for myself," she said ironically, implying that she did everything for him and only in this way could she forbid him the right to protest. He frowned and stayed silent. He felt that the lie surrounding him was now so entangled it was difficult to sort it out at all.

Everything she did for him was done entirely for her own sake, and she told him she was doing for her own sake what she actually was doing for her own sake, as though this was so improbable that he was bound to understand the opposite.

Certainly the eminent doctor did arrive at half past eleven. Once again there were tappings and listenings and significant conversations about the blind gut in his presence and in the next room, and questions and answers with such loaded looks that once again, instead of the real question of life and death which was now the only thing confronting him, the question that emerged was about his kidney and the blind gut which were doing something they shouldn't be doing, and how Mikhail Danilovitch and the eminence were about to pounce on them, this very minute, and force them to behave.

The eminent doctor said good-bye with a serious but not unhopeful expression. And at Ivan Ilyich's timid inquiry, his raised eyes shining with terror and hope, whether there was any chance of recovery, the doctor replied that one could not promise anything but there was a possibility. Ivan Ilyich followed the doctor out of the room with such a pitifully hopeful look, Praskovya Feodorovna even started crying when she saw it. She left the room to pay the eminent doctor his fee.

His spirits were lifted by the doctor's encouragement only for a little while. Once again it was the same room, the same pictures, curtains, wallpaper, medicine bottles, and the same aching, suffering body. And

Ivan Ilyich started groaning; he was given an injection, and lost consciousness.

When he came to, dusk was falling. They brought him his dinner. He forced himself to drink a little broth; and it was all the same again and another night was falling.

After dinner, at seven o'clock, Praskovya Feodorovna came into his room in evening attire, with plump, corseted breasts and traces of powder on her face. That very morning she had reminded him of their trip to the theater. Sarah Bernhardt[32] was in town, and at his insistence they had taken a box. Now he had forgotten about it, and her finery jarred on him. But he hid his irritation when he remembered that he himself had insisted they should order a box and go, because it would be an improving aesthetic experience for the children.

Praskovya Feodorovna came in well pleased with herself, but a little guiltily. She sat down beside him, asked how he felt—as he could see, in order to ask the question, not to find out the reply, knowing well enough there was nothing to find out—and started saying what was on her mind: that of course she wouldn't have dreamt of going, but the box was booked, and Hélène and her daughter, and Petrishev (the examining magistrate, his daughter's intended) were coming, and it would be quite impossible to allow them to go on their own. Of course she would have preferred so much more to sit with him. Only he must follow the doctor's orders while she was out.

"Oh yes, and Feodor Petrovich" (the suitor) "wanted to drop in. May he? And Liza."

"Let them come in."

In came his daughter, décolleté, her young body bared. His body made him suffer so. And she was putting hers on display. Strong, healthy, in love, impatient of illness, suffering, and death, which interfered with her happiness.

In came Feodor Petrovich in tails, his hair curled à la Capoul,[33] with long stringy neck richly enfolded in a white collar, huge white shirtfront, strong thighs tightly encased in black trousers, long white glove drawn over one hand, and opera hat.

After them, in his turn, the young schoolboy crept in unobtrusively, in his miniature new uniform, poor little thing, and gloves, with dreadful shadows under his eyes whose meaning was obvious to Ivan Ilyich.

He always felt sorry for his boy. And the boy's frightened look of pity was terrible for him. Apart from Gerasim, it seemed to Ivan Ilyich that only Vasya understood and pitied him.

Everyone sat down and inquired once again about his health. A silence fell. Liza asked her mother about the opera glasses. An altercation between mother and daughter followed about who had put them where. It became unpleasant.

Feodor Petrovich asked Ivan Ilyich whether he had ever seen Sarah Bernhardt. At first Ivan Ilyich did not understand what he was being asked, and then said, "No; have you seen her?"

"Yes, in *Adrienne Lecouvreur.*"[34]

Praskovya Feodorovna said she had been particularly good in that. Her daughter disagreed. A conversation started about the elegance and realism of Bernhardt's acting—that same old talk that is always one and the same.

In the middle of the conversation Feodor Petrovich glanced at Ivan Ilyich and fell silent. The others looked and fell silent. He was staring straight in front of him with glittering eyes, obviously exasperated by them. This had to be put right, but it was quite impossible to put it right. Somehow the silence had to be broken. Nobody could pluck up courage; everyone was on edge that the polite lie would be blown and they would all have to face up to what was right in front of them. Liza was the first to take the plunge. She broke the silence. She wanted to hide what everyone was feeling, but she got the words wrong.

"Well, if *it's time to go,* it's time to go," she said, glancing at her watch,[35] a gift from her father, and, barely perceptibly, smiled significantly at the young man about something only he knew about. She got up, her dress rustling.

Everyone got up, made their farewells, and left.

When they had gone out, Ivan Ilyich thought he felt easier. There were no lies; the lies had gone with them, but the pain remained. Always the same pain, always the same terror, making nothing easier, nothing more burdensome. Everything worse.

Once again minute followed minute, hour by hour, still the same, still without an end, and the inevitable end still more terrifying.

"Yes, send Gerasim here," he said in answer to Piotr's question.

9

His wife returned late that night. She came in on tiptoe, but he heard her, opened his eyes, and hastily shut them again. She wanted to send Gerasim out and sit with him herself. He opened his eyes and said, "No. Go."

"Are you suffering a lot?"

"It doesn't matter."

"Take some opium."

He consented and drank it. She went away.

He was in an oppressive state of unconsciousness till three in the morning. It seemed to him that he and his pain were being painfully pushed into a long, narrow black sack, pushed in deeper and deeper, and yet could not be pushed right through. And this terrible business is agonizing for him. He is both afraid, and wants to fall through; he struggles against it, and he tries to help. And suddenly he tore free, and fell, and came to himself. There is Gerasim, sitting as usual at the foot of the bed, dozing peacefully and patiently. And there he is, lying with his emaciated, stockinged feet resting on Gerasim's shoulders; there is the same shaded candle, and the same interminable pain.

"Go away, Gerasim," he whispered.

"It doesn't matter; I'll sit awhile."

"No, do go."

He drew his legs down, lay sideways on his arm, and felt sorry for himself. He waited till Gerasim went next door, abandoned all restraint, and cried like a child. He was crying for his helplessness, his terrible loneliness, people's cruelty, God's cruelty, the absence of God.

Why have You done all this? Why did You bring me here? What have I done that You torment me so dreadfully?

He did not even expect an answer, and cried because there was no answer, and could be no answer. The pain rose up again, but he did not stir and did not call out. He said to himself, Go on, batter me! But what for? What have I done to You? What is it for?

Then he grew quiet, stopped crying and even breathing, and grew all attention, as though he were listening not to a voice speaking in sounds but the voice of his soul, the train of thoughts rising inside him.

"What do you want?" was the first clear notion he heard which could be put into words. What do you want? What do you need? he repeated to himself. What? "Not to suffer. To live," he replied.

And again he gave himself over to such tense attention that even his pain did not distract him.

"Live? Live how?" asked the voice of his soul.

"Yes, live like I did before; well, and pleasantly."

"Like you lived before, well, and pleasantly?" asked the voice. And in his imagination he began going over the best moments of his pleasant life. But—how strange—all those best moments of his pleasant life now seemed quite different from what they had then seemed. Everything, except the first memories of his childhood. There, in his childhood, was something really pleasant that you could live with, if it were to come again. But the person who had experienced that happy time was no more: it was like a memory of another person.

As soon as those things began that resulted in Ivan Ilyich, the man he was now, so all those apparent joys melted away before his eyes, turning into something trivial and often bad. And the further he went from his childhood, the nearer he came to the present, the more trivial and dubious his pleasures became. It began with law school. There was still something genuinely good there; there was enjoyment, there was friendship, there were hopes. But in the final years these good moments already grew rarer. Then, in his service at the Governor's, good moments reappeared again; they were memories of love for women. Then it all became confused, and there was still less that was good. Further on, even less was good, and the further he went the less good it became.

Marriage...so accidental, and then disillusion, and the smell of his wife's breath, and the sensuality and hypocrisy! And that deathly job, and those anxieties about money, and one year like that, and two, and ten, and twenty, and all the same. And the further you went, the more deathly it became. Exactly as though I was steadily walking down a mountain, and thinking I was climbing it. And so I was. In public opinion I was climbing up, and at just the same rate life was slipping away from under me.... It's all up now—time to die!

So what is this? What is it for? It can't be. Surely it can't be that my life was so pointless, so wrong? And if it was that wrong and that pointless, then why die, and die in pain? Something's not right here.

"Maybe I didn't live as I should?" suddenly came into his head. "But how could that be, when I did everything as it should be done?" he said to himself, immediately driving off this, the one solution to the whole riddle of life and death, as though it were utterly out of the question.

"Now what do you want? To live? Live how? Live as you lived in court, when the usher called: The court is in session!" The court is coming, the judge is coming,[36] he repeated to himself. Here he comes, the judge! "But I'm not to blame!" he cried out bitterly. "What is my guilt?" And he stopped crying and, turning his face to the wall, started thinking about one thing and only one: What for? Why the misery?

But however much he thought, he could not find an answer. And whenever the thought came to him, as it often did, that everything stemmed from his not living as he should have done, he immediately remembered all the propriety of his life and pushed away such a bizarre idea.

10

Another two weeks passed. Ivan Ilyich no longer got up from his divan. He did not want to go to his bed but lay on the divan. Lying nearly all the time with his face to the wall, he continued to suffer alone the same inexplicable sufferings and thought the same insoluble thought. "What is this? Can it truly be death?" And his inner voice replied, "Yes, truly." "What is the agony for?" And the voice replied, "Just because, no reason." Other than this, beyond this, there was nothing.

From the very beginning of his illness, ever since Ivan Ilyich visited the doctor for the first time, his life split into two opposing and alternating moods: either despair and the expectation of incomprehensible and terrible death, or hope and the absorbing scrutiny of his bodily functions. Either his eyes were filled with the kidney or the gut, which had temporarily suspended their duties, or there was nothing but incomprehensible, unbearable death, which was impossible to escape.

These two states of mind had alternated from the very beginning of his illness, but the further the illness progressed, the more fantastical and suspect grew the idea of the kidney and the more real his awareness of approaching death.

He only needed to remember what he had been three months ago, and what he now was—to remember how steadily he kept walking down the mountain—and any possibility of hope was shattered.

In the last days of loneliness, when he found himself lying with his face to the back of the divan, utterly alone in the many-peopled city with its innumerable friends and families, a loneliness which could not have been more complete, nowhere, not on the ocean floor nor deep in the earth—in the last days of this dreadful loneliness Ivan Ilyich lived only in his imagination of the past. One after another, pictures of his past presented themselves. They always began with the most recent in time, and led back to the most distant, to his childhood, and there they stopped. If he remembered the stewed prunes that had been offered him today, then there came to mind the moist, wrinkled French plums of his childhood, their particular taste and the rush of saliva when you sucked them down to the stone. And alongside this memory of taste a whole line of other memories of that time rose up—his *nyanya*,[37] his brother, his toys. "I mustn't think of that, it hurts too much," Ivan Ilyich would say to himself, and heave himself back into the present. The button on the back of the leather divan, the wrinkles in the morocco. "Morocco is expensive but flimsy; we had a quarrel about it. But there was another morocco, and another quarrel, when we tore our father's briefcase and were punished, but Mamma brought us cakes." Once again it came to rest in his childhood, once again it hurt, and once more Ivan Ilyich tried to drive off the memory and think of other things.

And again, just here, together with this train of thought, there was another sequence of memories running through him, how his illness had strengthened and grown. And again, the further back he went, the more life there was. There was more kindness in his life, and more of life itself. And the one thing and the other ran into each other. "Just as my suffering grows worse and worse now, so the whole of my life went worse and worse," he thought. There was one spot of light far back, at the beginning of his life, and then it got blacker and blacker and quicker and quicker. "Inversely proportional to the square of its distance from death," thought Ivan Ilyich. And the image of a stone hurtling down with increasing speed plummeted deep into his soul. Life, a sequence of ever-increasing sufferings, hurtles faster and faster to its end, to the most appalling suffering. "I'm falling...." He jolted, stirred, and wanted to resist; but he knew already that he could not resist, and once again stared at the back of the divan with eyes that were tired of staring but unable not to stare at what was in front of them. And he waited, waited for that terrifying fall, the shock of impact, and the shattering. "I can't resist," he said to himself, "but if only I could understand what it's for? And that's impossible. It could only be explained if one could say I hadn't lived as I should. But that is quite inadmissible," he said to himself, remembering his law-abiding, correct, and proper life. "To accept that would be quite impossible," he said to himself, compressing his lips in an ironic smile, as though someone could see it and be taken in by it. "There is no explanation! Suffering, death... for what?"

11

Two weeks passed in this way. During this time an event occurred that Ivan Ilyich and his wife both desired: Petrishev made a formal proposal. It happened in the evening. The next day Praskovya Feodorovna went in to her husband, wondering how to tell him about Feodor Petrovich's proposal, but the same night Ivan Ilyich had suffered another change for the worse. Praskovya Feodorovna found him on the divan in a new position. He was lying on his back, moaning, and staring fixedly in front of him.

She started talking about medicines. He shifted his gaze to her. She did not finish what she had begun—such hatred, specifically for her, was in that look.

"For the love of Christ, let me die in peace," he said.

She wanted to go out, but at that moment his daughter came in and went up to him to say good morning. He looked at his daughter as he had at his wife, and in reply to her questions about his health, dryly replied that they would soon be free of him. Both fell silent, sat awhile, and went out.

"How are we to blame?" Liza asked her mother. "It's just as though we were doing it to him! I'm sorry for Papa, but why should we be made miserable?"

The doctor arrived at the usual time. Ivan Ilyich answered him yes and no, not lowering his baleful stare, and toward the end he said, "You know perfectly well you can do nothing, so leave it alone."

"We can alleviate your suffering," said the doctor.

"Not even that. Leave it."

The doctor went out into the drawing room and informed Praskovya Feodorovna that things were very bad, and only opium could lessen his pain, which must be intense.

The doctor said his physical suffering was intense, and that was true, but his spiritual suffering was worse, and that was what tormented him most of all.

His spiritual suffering lay in the fact that during the night, looking at Gerasim's kind, sleepy face with its high cheekbones, it suddenly occurred to him: what if in reality the whole of my life, my conscious life, was "not done"—"not the right thing"?[38]

It occurred to him that what had previously seemed to him a downright impossibility, that he had lived his whole life not as he should, could actually be true. It occurred to him that his barely recognized promptings to fight against what people in the highest positions deemed good, faintly perceptible impulses which he had promptly shrugged off—it could be these that were the reality, and all the rest was not the right thing. And his work, and the construction of his life, and his family, and those social and professional interests—all of them might be not the right thing. He tried to defend all these things to himself. And suddenly felt all the feebleness of what he was defending. And there was nothing to defend.

"And if this is so," he said to himself, "and I am leaving life in the knowledge that I have ruined everything that was given me, and it can't be put right, then what?" He lay flat on his back and started reconsidering his life in a completely different way. In the morning, when he saw the footman, and then his wife, and then his daughter, and then the doctor—their every movement and every word confirmed for him the dreadful truth that had come to him in the night. He saw himself in them, everything he had lived by, and saw clearly that all of it was not the right thing, all of it was a dreadful, vast lie heaped over life and death. This realization increased his sufferings, multiplied them tenfold. He groaned and thrashed about and tore at the bedclothes, which seemed to be choking him. And for this he hated them all.

They gave him a heavy dose of opium and he lost consciousness, but at dinnertime it all started again. He drove everyone away and turned restlessly from side to side.

His wife came to him and said, "Jean, sweetest, do this for me." (For me?) "It can't do any harm, and it often helps. Come on, it's nothing. Healthy people often—"

He opened his eyes wide.

"What? Take communion? What for? There's no need. And yet..."

She started crying.

"Will you? My dear friend? I'll send for our priest, he's so nice."

"Excellent, very good," he said.

When the priest came and heard his confession, he was softened, and felt a kind of ease from his doubts and consequently from his sufferings, and a moment's hope came to him. He started thinking again about his blind gut and the possibility of putting it right. He took the sacrament with tears in his eyes.

When they laid him down again after the sacrament, he felt better for a moment, and his hope of life rose again. He started thinking about the operation he had been offered. "To live, I want to live," he said to himself. His wife came to congratulate him; she said the conventional greeting, and added, "It's true, isn't it? You're better?"

Without looking at her, he said, "Yes."

Her clothes, the way she was put together, the expression on her face, the sound of her voice—everything said one thing to him: "Not the right thing. Everything you once lived by and now live by is a lie, a fraud, hiding life and death from you." And as soon as he thought that, his gall rose and with the gall agonizing physical suffering and with the suffering the knowledge of inevitable, imminent death. And something new started, a screwing, shooting pain and strangulated breathing.

The expression on his face when he uttered "yes" was dreadful. Saying that "yes," looking her straight in the eyes, he threw himself facedown extraordinarily quickly, considering how weak he was, and cried out, "Go away! Get out! Let me be!"

12

From that minute began the three days of unremitted screaming, so dreadful it could not be heard beyond two closed doors without horror. The moment he answered his wife, he understood that he was lost, there was no return, the end had come, the very end, but still his doubt had not been resolved and remained a doubt.

"Oh!" he cried in various intonations. "Ouh! Ouuuh!" He had started by screaming, "no!" and went on screaming "ouuuh."

Throughout those three days, when time had ceased to exist for him, he floundered in the black sack that an unseen, irresistible power was forcing him into. He struggled as a man condemned to death struggles in the hands of the executioner, knowing he cannot save himself, and with every minute he felt that in spite of all his labor, he was coming closer and closer to the thing that terrified him. He felt his agony came from his being thrust into the black hole, and even more from his inability to crawl into it. And the belief that his life had been good prevented him crawling into it. It was this very justification of his life that plucked him back, held him tight, and tormented him most of all.

Suddenly some kind of force jolted him in the chest, in his side, stifled his breath even harder; he tumbled into the hole, and there, at the end of it, something glimmered. He experienced that sensation he sometimes got in a railway carriage, when you think you are moving forward while actually going backward, and suddenly realize your true direction.

"Yes, it was all wrong," he said to himself, "but that doesn't matter. It can be done, it can. But what is *it*?" he asked himself, and suddenly grew still.

This was on the third day, an hour before his death. Just then the little schoolboy crept into his father's room and came up to his bed. The dying man was still screaming desperately and throwing his arms about. His hand fell on the boy's head. The boy caught hold of it, pressed it to his lips, and burst into tears.

It was just at this point that Ivan Ilyich fell through, saw the glimmer of light, and it became clear to him that his life had not been what it should have been, but that it could still be put right. He asked himself, what is *it*, and fell still, listening. Here he felt someone kissing his hand. He opened his eyes and glanced at his son. He felt sorry for him. His wife came up to him. He glanced at her. She was gazing at him with a look of despair on her face, her mouth open, unwiped tears on her nose and cheeks. He felt sorry for her.

"Yes, I'm making them miserable," he thought. "They're sorry for me, but it will be better for them when I'm dead." He wanted to say that, but didn't have the strength. "Besides, why talk? I must just do it," he thought. He glanced at his wife, indicating his son, and said, "Take him out ... sorry for him ... for you...." He wanted to add *prosti*, "forgive me," but said *propusti*, "let me pass," and, lacking the strength to correct himself, gave up, knowing that the one who needed to know would understand him.

And suddenly it was clear to him that what had been exhausting him and would not leave him was suddenly leaving him, falling away on two sides and ten sides and all sides. He was sorry for them, he had to stop them suffering. Free them and free himself from all this pain. "How good and how simple," he thought. "And the pain?" he asked himself. "Where's it gone? Come on, where are you, pain?"

He started listening.

"Yes, there it is. Well, never mind, let it be."

"And death? Where is it?"

He sought his old, habitual fear of death and could not find it. Where was death? What death? There was no fear, because there was no death.

Instead of death there was light.

"So that's it!" he suddenly said aloud. "What joy!"

For him it all happened in a moment, and the meaning of that moment did not change. For those around him his agony continued two hours. Something was gurgling in his chest; his wasted body was twitching. Gradually the snoring gurgle came less frequently.

"It is finished!" someone above him said.

He heard these words and repeated them in his soul. "Death is finished," he said to himself. "There is no more death."

He drew the air into himself, stopped in mid breath, stretched, and died.

Sleigh at Yasnaya Polyana by Leonid Pasternak (1862–1945).

MASTER AND MAN

1

It happened in the seventies, the day after the winter festival of St. Nicholas.[1] There was a celebration in the parish, and the local landowner, Vassili Andreyich Brekhunov, a merchant of the Second Guild,[2] had to attend. First he had to go to church, where he was warden, and then he had to entertain his family and friends at home. But now the last guests had driven off. Vassili Andreyich promptly prepared to set out for a neighboring landowner to buy a forest he'd been haggling over for some time. He was in a hurry to get off, because he didn't want buyers from the town to snap up the bargain before him. The only reason why the young landowner was asking ten thousand rubles[3] for the woodland was because Vassili Andreyich was offering seven. And seven thousand was just a third of its real value. An even better price was possible, because the land lay in his area and there was a long-standing agreement among the local traders not to bargain up prices in someone else's patch. But Vassili Andreyich had found out that timber merchants from the town were also planning to negotiate for the Goriachkin woodland. He decided to set out at once and clinch his deal with the owner. So, as soon as the festival was over, he took seven hundred rubles out of his chest, added to them two thousand three hundred rubles from the church funds in his care,[4] and, having carefully counted the three thousand rubles and put them away in his wallet, he got ready to go.

Nikita, the only one of Vassili Andreyich's laborers not drunk that day, ran out to harness the horse. A habitual drinker, he was sober because he had drunk away his coat and leather boots on the eve of the last fast, and then sworn off alcohol and succeeded in keeping his word for two months. He was still sober, despite the temptation of everyone else drinking heavily during the first two days of the holiday.

Nikolai was a fifty-year-old peasant from the nearby village, "no householder," as people said of him, because he had spent the better part of his life out in service, rather than in his own home. He was valued everywhere for being hardworking, deft, and strong, and above all for his pleasant, kindly character. But he never settled down because a couple of times a year, and sometimes more often than that, he got drunk, and then, apart from drinking away the clothes off his back, he became quarrelsome and aggressive. Vassili Andreyich had also turned him out more than once, but took him back again, valuing his honesty, love of animals, and above all his cheapness. Vassili Andreyich didn't give Nikita the eighty rubles such a good worker deserved, but forty, paying it out randomly, either in cash, or more often in kind, in goods from his shop charged at a high rate.

Nikita's wife, Marfa, once a beautiful, feisty woman, was in charge of his home, his teenage son and two daughters. Nikita was not invited to live with her. She had been living for the last twenty years with a barrel maker, a peasant from another village who had settled himself in very nicely with her. And, in any case, however much she ordered her husband about when he was sober, she was terrified of him drunk. Once when he got really drunk at home, Nikita broke into his wife's chest and—presumably to pay her back for his submissiveness when sober—pulled out all her most valued possessions, took his axe, and diced her best smocks like a cucumber on the chopping block. Everything Nikita earned went to his wife, but he didn't object. Only two days before the festival Marfa came over to Vassili Andreyich to pick up white flour, sugar, and a half quart of vodka worth three rubles in all, as well as five rubles in cash, and thanked him for it as though it were a special kindness when in fact, at the lowest possible rate, Vassili Andreyich owed them at least twenty rubles.

"After all, what agreement did we ever make between us?" Vassili Andreyich used to say to Nikita. "If you need anything, take it. You can work it off later. I'm not like the others, making their men wait and then cooking up reckonings and fines. You serve me, and I won't let you down."

As he said this Vassili Andreyich honestly believed that he was doing Nikita a favor. He had the knack of speaking with such conviction that everyone relying on him financially—not least Nikita himself—went along with the fiction that he was doing his very best for them, not cheating them.

"Of course I understand, Vassili Andreyich, it's like working for my own father. I understand perfectly," Nikita replied, understanding perfectly clearly that Vassili Andreyich was cheating him but feeling at the same time that there was no point in trying to sort out their accounts. He should just go along with it, and take what he was given till he found work elsewhere.

Now, ready and cheerful as usual, Nikita followed his master's orders to harness up, and went with his pigeon-toed, springy, light step into the shed. Taking the heavy, tasseled leather bridle off its nail and jingling the rings of the bit, he went into the closed stall where the horse he was to harness stood on its own.

"Getting bored were you, honey?" Nikita replied to the horse's mild, welcoming whinny. He was a dark dappled bay stallion, of middling height with a sloping crupper, standing alone in his stall. "We're nearly there—let me water you first," he went on, talking to the horse exactly as we do to creatures that understand us, and, brushing his plump, dusty back with the skirt of his coat, he eased the bridle over the young bay's handsome head, freed his ears and mane, and slipping off his halter, led him out to drink.

Stepping delicately out of the byre heaped high with dung, Mukhorty[5] playfully kicked out with his hind leg as though trying to get at Nikita, running at a trot beside him to the water pump.

"Steady now, silly boy!" Nikita kept repeating, knowing very well how Mukhorty kicked out with his hind hoof—carefully, just to graze his muddy coattails, not hurt him. It was a trick Nikita was particularly fond of.

His thirst slaked by the icy water, the horse sighed. Wrinkling his strong wet lips, their hairs shedding transparent drops into the trough, he grew still as if deep in thought. Suddenly he snorted noisily.

"Well, if you don't want any more, don't have it. We'll understand; just don't ask again," Nikita said to Mukhorty in all seriousness, painstakingly making things clear. Taking him by the reins, he ran back to the barn, dragging the cheerful young bay frisking all the way across the yard.

There were no laborers about, only an outsider, the cook's husband, who had come for the festival.

"Go and ask what sledge they want harnessed, there's a good chap," said Nikita. "Is it the wide one or the tiddly one?"

The cook's husband went into the house with its iron roof and raised foundations and soon came back saying they wanted the little one. Meanwhile, Nikita had already put on Mukhorty's collar and brass-studded bellyband. Leading the horse by one hand, and carrying a light, painted wooden yoke in the other, he was on his way to the two sledges standing in the shed.

"If it's the tiddler, then it's the tiddler," he said, backing the intelligent horse, which kept pretending to bite him, into the shafts and harnessing him with the help of the cook's husband.

When everything was nearly ready, with only the reins to see to, Nikita sent the cook's husband to the stable for straw and to the barn for sacking.

"There we go, darling. Steady now, no nonsense," Nikita repeated to Mukhorty, cramming down into the sledge the freshly threshed oat straw the man brought him. "Now give me the bark ticking to tuck it in, and then we'll put the sacking over the top. There now, that'll be comfortable to sit on," he went on, doing as he said and tucking the sacking in all around the straw on the seat.

"There we are. Thanks again, old man," Nikita said to the cook's husband. "It's always easier with two." And, untangling the reins looped together by a ring, Nikita took his place on the driver's bench and set the kind horse, impatient to be gone, across the frozen manure to the yard gates.

"Uncle Nikit! Hey, uncle, uncle!" a thin little voice called behind him, and a seven-year-old boy in a short black sheepskin jacket, new white felt boots, and a warm hat ran hurriedly out of the house into the yard. "Take me, too," he begged, buttoning up his half jacket as he ran.

"Up you come then, sweetheart," said Nikita, pulling up. Making room for his master's pale, skinny boy who was now glowing with delight, he drove out into the road.

It was past two in the afternoon. The day was freezing—ten degrees below, overcast, and windy. Half the sky was covered by dark, low cloud. In the yard it was sheltered. But on the road you could feel the wind; snow was pouring off a nearby barn roof and whirling around in the corner by the bath house. As soon as Nikita drove out of the yard gates and turned his horse to the wing of the house, Vassili Andreyich came out of the entrance, cigarette in mouth, his sheepskin-lined overcoat tightly belted low on his hips, the trampled snow on the high porch squeaking under his leather-soled felt boots. He stopped, sucked the last drag of his cigarette, dropped it underfoot, and ground it out. Glancing aside at the horse and breathing smoke through his mustache, he tucked in the corners of his collar on either side of his ruddy, clean-shaven cheeks, so that the fur wouldn't get bedraggled by his breath.

"Well, what d'you know! There before me, are you?" he said, seeing his little boy in the sledge. Vassili Andreyich was lit up by the wine he had drunk with his guests and consequently extra satisfied by everything belonging to him and everything he did. The sight of his son, whom he always mentally called his heir, gave him huge pleasure at this moment. He looked at him, screwing up his eyes and showing his long teeth.

Vassili Andreyich's thin, pale, pregnant wife was standing behind him in the entrance to see him off. Her head and shoulders were wrapped up in a woolen shawl so that only her eyes could be seen.

"You really should take Nikita with you," she was saying as she came timidly out of the doorway.

Vassili Andreyich said nothing, and in response to her words, which were evidently not to his liking, frowned and spat crossly.

"You're taking money with you," his wife persisted in the same plaintive voice. "And the weather might turn bad, God forbid."

"So I don't know the way and have to take a guide with me?" Vassili Andreyich said through unnaturally tight lips, pronouncing each syllable with pointed precision, his habitual delivery when dealing with traders.

"No really, you should take him. For God's sake, please do," his wife repeated, winding her shawl the other way.

"Women! There's no contradicting them!⁶ What on earth should I take him for?"

"It's all right, Vassili Andreyich, I'm ready to come," said Nikita cheerfully. "It's just that the horses'll have to be fed without me," he added, turning to his mistress.

"I'll see to that, Nikitushka. I'll get Simyon to do it," she said.

"Well, shall we go then, Vassili Andreyich?" Nikita asked, waiting.

"Seems we have to humor the missus. But if you are coming with me, go and get a warmer coat on," said Vassili Andreyich, smiling again and winking at Nikita's short coat, ripped in the armpits, torn across the back, frayed to a fringe along the hem, the sloppy, soiled witness to a lifetime's labor.

"Hey, old chap, come and hold the horse for a minute!" Nikita shouted to the cook's husband in the yard.

"Let me, let me!" squealed the boy, pulling his frozen little red hands out of his pockets and seizing the cold reins.

"No need to primp over that coat of yours, just hurry up!" Vassili Andreyich called out teasingly.

"In a jiffy, Vassili Andreyich," said Nikita. Pigeon-toed in his old, felt-soled *valenki*,⁷ he quickly ran across the yard to the servants' quarters.

"Come on, Arinushka, give me my coat off the stove—I'm to go with the master," he said, bursting into the hut and snatching his cloth belt off its nail.

The cook, fresh from her after-dinner nap, was heating the samovar for her husband. Nikita's haste was infectious. Bustling like him, with a cheery greeting, she seized his shabby kaftan from where it was drying on the stove and hurriedly started shaking out the coarse, crumpled cloth.

"So you'll be getting a good bit of time off with your husband," Nikita said to her. He was so good-natured and sympathetic, he always had a kind word for whoever he was with. And, drawing his narrow, frayed belt around him, he sucked in his already skinny stomach and pulled it as tight as he could around his short sheepskin coat.

"There we go," he said, speaking now not to the cook but to his belt, tucking in its ends; "you can't come undone like that," and, shrugging his shoulders up and down to loosen the sleeves, he put on his kaftan, flexed his back to free his arms, slapped under his armpits, and picked his gloves off the shelf. "That'll do."

"You should wrap your feet up," the cook said to him. "Your boots are no good."

Nikita stopped, as if he'd just remembered.

"Yes, I should.... Well, it'll do as it is; it's not far."

And he ran out into the yard.

"Won't you be cold, Nikitushka?" asked his mistress, when he got to the sledge.

"It's not a bit cold; I'm really warm," said Nikita, rearranging the straw in the sledge, ready to cover his legs when he got in, and stowing the whip under the straw. There was no need for a whip on Mukhorty.

Vassili Andreyich was already on the seat, almost filling the body of the sledge with his broad back, clad in two fur-lined greatcoats. Taking the reins at once, he flicked the horse. Nikita jumped on as they moved off and squeezed himself in at his master's left, with one leg hanging out.

2

With a light squeak of runners, they set off at a brisk pace down the smooth, icy village street.

"What are you doing, back there? Give me the whip, Nikita!" shouted Vassili Andreyich, evidently well pleased by his son and heir, who was trying to hang on by the runners at the back of the sledge. "You've got it coming to you! Young puppy! Run home to your mummy, scamp!"

The boy dropped off. Mukhorty quickened his pace and went into a trot.

Vassili Andreyich's house was in Kresti, a village of six houses. As soon as they had passed the blacksmith's, the last in the street, they realized the wind was much stronger than they had thought. The road was already almost invisible. The tracks of their sledge runners were instantly blown over with snow, and you could only make out the road because it was higher than the surrounding ground. The fields were a whirl of snow, and the line between earth and sky couldn't be seen. Telyatin's forest, always a clear landmark, loomed fleetingly through the dust of snow. The wind blew from the left, persistently streaming to one side the mane on Mukhorty's sleek, straight neck and tossing sideways his thick tail tied in a single knot. Nikita's broad collar was plastered against his face and nose because he sat on the windward side.

"It's too snowy to put him through his paces properly," said Vassili Andreyich, proud of his lively horse. "I rode him to Pashutino in half an hour once."

"What?" said Nikita, who couldn't hear for his collar.

"To Pashutino, I said, he got there in half an hour," Vassili Andreyich shouted.

"No question he's a good horse," Nikita replied.

They fell silent. But Vassili Andreyich wanted to talk.

"Well, I suppose you've told your wife to get her cooper off the drink?" he began in the same loud voice, perfectly convinced Nikita would be flattered to chat with someone as important and clever as himself, and so pleased with his little pleasantry, it didn't even occur to him that Nikita might find the subject distasteful.

Once again Nikita failed to catch his master's words that were carried away by the wind.

Vassili Andreyich repeated his joke about the barrel maker in his loud, precise voice.

"God be with them, Vassili Andreyich. I don't meddle in their affairs. As long as she doesn't ill-treat my boy, let be."

"Yes indeed," said Vassili Andreyich, and started a new tack. "Well, what d'you think, will you be buying a new horse in the spring?"

"Yes, I'll have to," said Nikita, holding back his collar and bending over to his master.

Now the conversation interested him, and he wanted to hear everything.

"My kid's growing up; he'll have to start plowing—we used to hire help," he said.

"Well, why don't you take the skinny one? I won't ask much for him," Vassili Andreyich shouted, in his animation turning to the one all-consuming interest that occupied all his thoughts—how to make a profit.

"Or you could give me just fifteen rubles, not more, and I'd get one at the horse fair," said Nikita, knowing the horse his master wanted to palm off on him was worth no more than seven, but once Vassili Andreyich had given it to him in lieu of wages, he'd value it at twenty-five, and that meant half a year's wages gone.

"It's a good horse. I'll deal with you as I would for myself. On my honor. Brekhunov never cheated anyone.[8] I'd rather lose out myself than be like the others. On my word," Vassili Andreyich shouted, in the voice he used to swindle his customers. "A fine horse!"

"No doubt," said Nikita with a sigh, and, certain there was nothing more worth hearing, let go of his collar, which instantly covered his ear and face.

They drove on in silence for half an hour. The wind bit sharply into Nikita's side and arm, where his coat was torn.

He hugged himself and breathed into the collar covering his mouth, and seemed to feel less cold.

"Well, what d'you think, should we go through Karamishevo or direct?" asked Vassili Andreyich.

The way through Karamishevo was by a busier road, marked with two rows of high stakes, but it took a longer way around. The direct route was shorter, but it was rarely used and had either no markers at all or poor ones that were snowed under.

Nikita thought a little.

"Through Karamishevo may be longer but it's better going," he decided.

"But if we go straight there's only the hollow to pass without losing the road, and then by the forest it's easy going," said Vassili Andreyich, who wanted to go straight.

"As you wish," said Nikita, letting go of his collar again.

Vassili Andreyich did as he wanted. After half a kilometer they turned left by a tall, upended oak branch bending in the wind, a few dry leaves still clinging to it.

The turn brought the wind almost full in their faces. A light snow began to fall. Vassili Andreyich was driving, puffing out his cheeks and breathing through his mustache. Nikita was dozing.

They drove in silence for ten minutes or so. Suddenly Vassili Andreyich began saying something.

"What?" said Nikita, opening his eyes.

Vassili Andreyich didn't answer, bending around and looking behind him and in front, ahead of the horse. Mukhorty's coat was curly with sweat on his neck and withers. He went at a walking pace.

"What is it, I said?" Nikita repeated.

"What? What?" Vassili Andreyich mocked him angrily. "No markers to be seen! We must have lost the road."

"Then stop a minute and I'll find it," said Nikita. Jumping lightly off the sledge and taking out the whip from under the straw, he went left from his side of the sledge.

That year the snow wasn't deep, so that you could drive everywhere, but all the same it was knee-deep in places and got into Nikita's boots. He felt his way with his feet and the whip, but the road was nowhere to be found.

"Well?" asked Vassili Andreyich when he got back to the sledge.

"Nothing this side. I'll have to feel about on the other side."

"There's something dark over there. Go and have a look," said Vassili Andreyich.

Nikita made his way over to the dark thing. It was earth which the wind had blown from the bare fields of winter oats, blackening the snow. Having trudged about on the right as well, Nikita came back, beat the snow off himself, shook out his boots, and sat down in the sledge.

"We must drive to the right," he said decisively. "The wind came at my left, and now it's right in my face. Turn right," he repeated firmly.

Vassili Andreyich obeyed and turned to the right. But there was still no road. They drove on like that for a while. The wind didn't slacken, and it was snowing lightly.

"Well, it looks like we've completely lost the road, Vassili Andreyich," Nikita said suddenly and, it seemed, with some satisfaction. "What's that?" he added, pointing to a black potato stalk poking out of the snow.

Vassili Andreyich stopped Mukhorty, who was in a sweat and breathing heavily.

"What's what?" he asked.

"We're on the Zakharov lands, that's what. That's where we've got to!"

"Rubbish!"

"It's not rubbish, Vassili Andreyich; I'm telling the truth," said Nikita. "You can tell from the sound of the runners, too—we're driving over a potato field, and that's the stalks, heaped over there, where they've cleared the stubble. It's the Zakharov factory land."

"Good Lord, how badly we've gone astray!" said Vassili Andreyich. "What should we do?"

"Just go straight, we'll get out somewhere," said Nikita. "If not at Zakharovka, then we'll get to the owner's farm."

Vassili Andreyich did as he was told and set Mukhorty off in Nikita's direction. They went on like that for some time. Sometimes they drove onto bare fields and the runners grated over frozen lumps of earth. Sometimes they got into stubble land, winter crops, or fields sown for spring, where stalks of straw and wormwood poked out of the snow, shaken by the wind. Sometimes they ran into deep snow, lying uniformly white and even, above which nothing could be seen.

Snow fell from above and sometimes rose from underfoot.[9] Mukhorty was clearly exhausted, going at a walk, his sweaty coat all curly and white with rime. Suddenly he stumbled and plunged down into a ditch or small watercourse. Vassili Andreyich wanted to pull him back, but Nikita shouted, "Don't pull him! If we're in we'll have to climb out. Come on, sweetheart, come on, darling," he cried out cheerfully to the horse, jumping out of the sledge and vanishing in his turn into the ditch.

Mukhorty took it at a run and quickly got himself back onto the icy bank. Evidently it was a man-made trench.

"Where on earth are we?" asked Vassili Andreyich.

"We'll soon find out," Nikita replied. "Let's go; we'll come out somewhere."

"Isn't that the Goriachkin forest?" said Vassili Andreyich, pointing to something dark, visible in the snow ahead.

"We'll just drive up and see what sort of forest it is," said Nikita.

He could see long, dry willow leaves driven by the wind from whatever was dark ahead, so he knew it must be some kind of settlement, not a forest—but he was reluctant to say so. True enough, they had driven barely two hundred meters beyond the ditch before dark trees showed up ahead and a doleful new sound could be heard. Nikita had guessed correctly; it was no forest but a row of tall willows, still tossing a few leaves. Evidently they had been planted along the trench of a threshing ground. When they drove up to the willows, sighing drearily in the wind, Mukhorty suddenly planted his forefeet higher than the sledge, got his hind legs up the rise as well, turned left, and stopped floundering up to his knees in snow. They had found a road.

"Well, we've arrived," said Nikita, "but goodness knows where."

The horse kept going straight along the road. After less than a kilometer they saw the straight line of a threshing barn's dark wattle wall, its roof thickly coated with snow pouring continually over the edge. Skirting the barn, the road turned into the wind, and they ran into a snowdrift. But ahead they could see a lane between two houses. Evidently the snow had drifted down the lane and would have to be crossed. Sure enough, once over that, they came out into the village street. In the yard of the last house frozen washing still hung out. Two shirts, one red and one white, trousers, foot cloths and a petticoat flapped furiously on the line. The white shirt looked particularly despairing, shaking its arms and struggling.

"Just look, a lazy housewife, or a dead one, not taking her washing in before the holiday," said Nikita, eyeing the fluttering shirts.

3

It was still windy at the end of the street, and the road was drifted over with snow, but in the middle of the village it grew quiet, warm, and cheery. A dog was barking in one yard. In another, a woman with her skirts wrapped around her head ran across to the door of her hut, pausing on the threshold to stare at the strangers. From the depths of the village girls' voices could be heard singing.

There was less wind, snow, and frost here, it seemed.

"But this is Grishkino!" said Vassili Andreyich.

"So it is," Nikita replied.

It really was Grishkino, which meant they had drifted too far left and traveled about eight kilometers not quite in the right direction. Still, they had made some headway. It was about another five from Grishkino to Goriachkin.

In the middle of the village they came across a tall fellow walking down the middle of the street.

"Who's that?" he cried, stopping the horse, and, instantly recognizing Vassili Andreyich, took hold of the shaft, felt along it hand over hand till he got to the sledge and perched on the seat.

It was an old acquaintance of Vassili Andreyich, the peasant Isai, well known as the best horse thief in the district.

"Hey! Vassili Andreyich! What brings you here?" said Isai, breathing vodka over Nikita.

"We were on our way to Goriachkin."

"Good God, how you've missed your way! You should have made for Malakhovo."

"Too bad what we should have done, we didn't manage it," said Vassili Andreyich, reining in Mukhorty.

"That's a nice little horse," said Isai, glancing at the bay and tightening the knot high in his thick tail with a practiced hand. "Going to stay the night then, are you?"

"No way, brother, we absolutely must get on."

"Needs must, then. And who's that? Ha! Nikita Stepanich!"

"Who else?" said Nikita. "Tell me, there's a good soul, how should we keep to the road this time?"

"No need to get lost! Turn back, go straight down the road, and when you come out of the village keep straight. Don't take the left turn. You'll come out onto the highway, then turn right."

"Which turn do we take off the high road—the winter way or the summer one?" Nikita asked.

"Take the winter one. As soon as you come out onto the highway there are some little bushes, and opposite them there's a marker, a big twiggy oak branch. That's it."

Vassili Andreyich turned the horse to drive back through the village.

"Better stay the night!" Isai shouted behind them.

But Vassili Andreyich didn't answer and flicked the reins. Five kilometers on a good road, two of them through forest, would be no problem, particularly now that the wind appeared to have dropped and the snow was easing off.

They went back down the trampled village street, its snow discolored here and there by fresh dung, past the yard with the washing where the white shirt had torn itself free and was hanging by one frozen arm, and drove out to the dreadfully moaning line of willows. Once again they found themselves in open country. Far from slackening, the snowstorm seemed to have got even stronger. The road was completely snowed under, and you could only tell you weren't going wrong by the roadside markers. But even the stakes just ahead were hard to see, because the wind blew straight into their faces.

Vassili Andreyich was screwing up his eyes, bending his head forward, looking out for stakes, but mostly he gave the horse its head, putting his trust in him. Sure enough, Mukhorty didn't lose his way but kept going, turning this way and that as the road demanded, feeling it under his hooves, so that even though the snow and wind grew stronger, the stakes continued to appear to their left and right.

They went on like that for about ten minutes, when suddenly something dark appeared in front of them, moving through the slanting net of wind-driven snow. It was a group of fellow travelers. Mukhorty caught up to them and knocked against the sledge in front with his forelegs.

"Go ahe-e-ead!" they shouted from the other sledge.

Vassili Andreyich started to overtake them. There were three peasants and a woman sitting in the sledge, evidently visitors returning from the festival. One was lashing the snow-covered rump of their little horse with a switch. Two others, waving their arms, were shouting something from the front. The woman, motionless, bundled up, and covered in snow, hunched in the back.

"Where are you from?" shouted Vassili Andreyich.

"From A-a-!" was all they could hear.

"Come again?"

"From A-a-a-a!" one of the peasants bellowed at the top of his voice, just as unintelligibly.

"Keep up! Don't let them past!" shouted the other, ceaselessly thwacking his little horse with the switch.

"From the festival, then?"

"Keep up, Syomka! Get on! Overtake them!"

The sledge runners knocked against each other and nearly locked, but broke loose again, and the peasants' sledge began to fall behind.

Their shaggy, potbellied horse was white with snow, stumbling on stumpy little legs through the deep drifts, vainly trying to run away from the thrashing switch. He was a young horse, clearly at the end of his tether, breathing heavily under the low shaft bow.

His lower lip was pulled back like a fish; his nostrils were flared and ears flattened with terror. This sight kept level by Nikita's shoulder for a few seconds, then dropped behind.

"That's drink for you," said Nikita. "They've done for that little horse. Barbarians!"

For a few moments the tormented horse's noisy breath and the drunken shouts of the peasants pursued them. The snuffled panting died away. Finally even the shouting couldn't be heard. Once again there was silence around them, only the wind hissing in their ears and the runners occasionally grating over bare patches of road.

The encounter had cheered and encouraged Vassili Andreyich. With growing confidence he urged Mukhorty on, relying on him and neglecting the guideposts.

Nikita had nothing to do but doze, as he always did when he could, catching up on many hours' lost sleep. Suddenly the horse stopped. Nikita jerked forward and nearly fell.

"Look here, the going's got bad again," said Vassili Andreyich.

"How's that?"

"There are no stakes to be seen. We must have got off the road again."

"If it's lost, we'll have to find it," Nikita said shortly. He got down to feel his way about in the snow once more, stepping lightly on his pigeon-toed feet.

He walked about for a long time, disappearing from view, reappearing and disappearing again. At last he came back.

"There's no road here; maybe it's somewhere ahead," he said, getting back on the sledge.

It was getting dark. The blizzard was no worse, but nor was it diminishing.

"If only we could hear those peasants," said Vassili Andreyich.

. "They haven't caught us up, see; we must've lost our way a long way back. Maybe they're lost too," said Nikita.

"But where should we go?" asked Vassili Andreyich.

"We must give the horse his head," said Nikita. "He'll get us there. Give me the reins."

Vassili Andreyich gave him the reins all the more willingly because his hands were beginning to freeze, even in his warm gloves.

Nikita took the reins and held them loosely, trying not to twitch them, delighting in his favorite. And indeed the clever horse, swiveling one ear and then the other from side to side, began to turn about.

"The only thing he can't do is talk," Nikita kept saying. "Look what he's doing! Go on, go on, clever clogs! That's it!"

The wind started blowing from behind and it grew warmer.

"And he's clever," Nikita went on, rejoicing in Mukhorty. "A Kirgiz nag is strong but stupid. But this one—look what he's doing with his ears. No telegraph for him! He can sense things a mile off."

And barely half an hour passed before something showed dark in front of them, whether forest or settlement, and on their right the stakes reappeared. They must have come out onto the road again.

"But this is Grishkino, all over again," Nikita suddenly remarked.

Sure enough, to their left was the same threshing barn with snow pouring off its roof, and further on was the familiar washing line with its frozen linen, shirts, and trousers, thrashing just as desperately in the wind.

Once more they came into the village and once more it grew quiet, warm, and cheery. The dung-strewn street came back into view. As before, they heard the sound of voices and singing, and a dog began barking. It was already so dark that lights were burning in some of the windows.

Halfway down the street Vassili Andreyich turned his horse toward a large house with walls two bricks thick, and stopped at the porch.

Nikita went up to the snowy window, drifting snowflakes glittering in its glow, and knocked with his whip.

"Who's that?" someone shouted in reply.

"Friends—Brekhunov, from Kresti. Come out a minute, could you?" Nikita answered.

The figure left the window, and a couple of minutes later they heard an inside door being pulled unstuck. The latch clacked in the outer door, and a tall old peasant with a white beard peered out, a half jacket thrown over his white holiday shirt, holding the door back against the wind. Behind him stood a young lad in a red shirt and leather boots.

"Is that really you, Andreyich?" said the old man.

"We've lost our way, brother," said Vassili Andreyich. "We wanted to get to Goriachkin, and landed up here. We drove off and got lost again."

"Good Lord, you have gone astray!" said the old man. "Petrushka, go and open the gates," he said to the lad in the red shirt.

"Right away," said the boy cheerfully and ran into the passage.

"But we won't stop," said Vassili Andreyich.

"You can't drive off again—it's dark now, stay the night."

"I'd be glad to stay, but we must get on. It's business, friend, I mustn't."

"Well, warm up a bit at least. The samovar's waiting," said the old man.

"A bit of warmth would be nice," said Vassili Andreyich. "It won't get any darker, and when the moon rises it'll get lighter. Shall we go in then, Nikit, and get warm?"

"Warm up a bit? Why not?" said Nikita, who was frozen and keen to thaw himself out.

Vassili Andreyich went into the house with the old man. Nikita drove through the gates opened by Petrushka and, guided by him, took the horse under the overhanging roof of the barn. The barn was heaped so high with dung, the horse's wooden yoke caught on the crossbeam. Some chickens and a cockerel already perched under the roof started clucking grumpily and scrabbled along the beam. The sheep shied away, their hooves tapping on the frozen dung. A frightened young dog whined miserably and barked angrily at the stranger.

Nikita talked to everyone. He apologized to the chickens and reassured them that he wouldn't disturb them again. He rebuked the sheep for getting frightened without knowing why, and kept soothing the dog while he tied up the horse.

"There, that's better," he said, slapping the snow off himself. "Listen to you barking!" he went on to the dog. "Quiet, silly! That's enough—you're just upsetting yourself. We're friends, not thieves."

"And they're what they call the three domestic advisers," said the lad, pushing the rest of the sledge under the overhang with a strong shove.

"What d'you mean, advisers?" asked Nikita.

"That's how it's printificated in Pullson[10]—the thief steals up to the house, the dog barks—meaning, keep your wits about you, look out! The cockerel crows—that means, get up! The cat washes itself and that means a dear friend is coming, get ready to entertain him!" said the boy, smiling.

Petrushka could read and knew his only book, Paulson's primer, almost by heart. Particularly when he was a bit drunk, like today, he loved quoting passages from it that seemed appropriate to him.

"That's right," said Nikita.

"Are you frozen, granddad?" Petrushka added.

"You could say that," said Nikita, and they crossed the yard to the house.

4

The farmstead which Vassili Andreyich had come to was one of the richest in the village. The family owned five holdings[11] and rented more land on the side. They had six horses in their yard, three cows, two calves, and some twenty sheep. They were a family of twenty-two: four married sons, six grandsons, of whom only Petrushka was married, two great-grandsons, three orphans, and four daughters-in-law with their children. It was one of the few farmsteads that had remained undivided, but here, too, the dull internal grumble of family strife, beginning as always among the womenfolk, would soon lead, swiftly and inevitably, to the division of the property. Two sons lived in Moscow as water carriers; another was in the army. At home now there was the old man and his wife, his second son—who was in charge of the homestead—and his oldest son, who had come from Moscow for the festival. Then there were all the wives and their children, and, apart from the family, a neighbor who was godfather to one of the children.

In the living quarters a shaded lamp hung above the table, brightly lighting the tea things, a bottle of vodka, and food below. It cast a glow on the brick walls, hung with icons in the holy corner, with pictures arranged on either side. Vassili Andreyich sat at the head of the table in just one short, black sheepskin, sucking in his frozen mustache and examining the people around him with his protuberant, hawklike eyes. As well as Vassili Andreyich, the bald, white-bearded old man, the head of the family, sat at the table in a white homespun shirt. Next to him was the son from Moscow, broad shouldered and brawny backed, in a thin cotton print shirt, and another broad-shouldered son, his younger brother[12] and the master of the household. Finally there was a skinny redheaded peasant, their neighbor.

The peasants, who'd had their vodka and a bite to eat, were just about to drink tea. The samovar was already humming on the floor by the oven. Children could be seen on top of the oven[13] and in the high bunks; on a lower bunk a woman bent by a cradle. The old man's wife, her face and even her lips crisscrossed with the finest wrinkles, was attending to Vassili Andreyich.

As Nikita came in, she was offering her guest some vodka which she had just poured into a thick glass tumbler.

"Don't refuse, Vassili Andreyich, you really mustn't; drink to our holiday," she was saying. "Do take a glass with us, dear."

The sight and smell of the vodka, especially now, when he was worn out and frozen through, thoroughly discomfited Nikita. He frowned and, shaking off the snow from his cap and kaftan, went over to the icons. As if not seeing anyone, he crossed himself three times and bowed to the icons, then, turning to the old man presiding, bowed first to him and then to everyone else at the table, then to the women standing by the oven, and said, "A happy holiday to you." He began to remove his outer clothes, keeping his eyes off the table.

"Well, haven't you got frosty, uncle!" said the older brother, looking at Nikita's face, eyebrows, and beard, all thick with snow.

Nikita took off his kaftan, shook it out again, hung it by the oven, and came up to the table. He was also offered vodka. There was a moment's painful struggle. He nearly took a tumbler and knocked back the clear, aromatic liquor. But, glancing at Vassili Andreyich, he remembered his oath, remembered his lost leather boots, remembered the cooper, thought of his son and the horse he had promised to buy him, sighed, and refused.

"I don't drink, thank you kindly," he said, frowning, and sat down on a bench by the second window.

"How's that?" asked the older brother.

"I just don't drink, that's all," said Nikita, keeping his eyes lowered. Squinting down at his sparse whiskers and beard, he started thawing off the icicles.

"It's not good for him," said Vassili Andreyich, chasing the glass he'd drunk with a bite of bread.

"Then take a glass of tea," said the old lady kindly. "You must be chilled to the bone, poor dear. What are you women dawdling about with that samovar?"

"It's ready," answered a young woman. Flicking the curtain over the samovar, which was now boiling over, she carried it across with difficulty, lifted it up, and bumped it onto the table.

Meanwhile Vassili Andreyich was describing how they had lost their way and come back to the same village twice, how they had strayed and the drunks they had met. Their hosts marveled and explained how and why they had gone wrong, who the drunkards had been, and told them exactly what road they should have taken.

"A baby could get from here to Molchanovka. It's only a matter of getting the right turn off the big road, where the bush is. You just didn't go far enough!" said the neighbor.

"You should stay the night. The women will make up a bed," the old lady urged.

"You could go in the morning; it would be much better," the old man agreed.

"I really can't, friend. Business calls," Vassili Andreyich said. "Lose an hour, and waste a year," he added, remembering the woodland and the dealers who might outbid him. "We will get there, won't we?" he said, turning to Nikita.

Nikita didn't reply for a long time, seemingly absorbed in thawing out his beard and mustache.

"If we don't lose the road again," he said somberly.

Nikita was gloomy because he desperately wanted some vodka, and the only other thing that could satisfy his craving was tea, which no one had yet given him.

"But it's only a matter of getting as far as the turnoff. We can't get lost after that—the forest takes us all the way there," said Vassili Andreyich.

"It's your business, Vassili Andreyich. If we're to go, then we'll go," said Nikita, taking the tea that was offered him.

"We'll drink up our tea, then, and be off."

Nikita said nothing, just nodded. Carefully pouring his tea into the saucer, he began warming his fingers, perpetually swollen from hard work, in the steam. Then, biting off a tiny bit of sugar, he bowed to his hosts, saying, "Your health," and sucked up the warm drink.

"If someone could only take us as far as the turn," said Vassili Andreyich.

"That's no problem," said the older son. "Petrushka will harness up and take you as far as that."

"Then do, brother, and I'll thank you."

"What nonsense, love!" said the kindly old woman. "Bless you, we're glad to help."

"Petrushka, go and harness the mare," said the older son.

"Right away," said Petrushka with a smile. Promptly snatching his cap from its nail, he ran out.

While the horse was being seen to, the conversation turned back to the subject Vassili Andreyich had interrupted by his arrival at the window. The old man was complaining to his neighbor, the village elder, about his third son, who had sent his father nothing for the festival, while the son's wife got a fine French shawl.

"There's no holding young people nowadays," said the old man.

"They've got completely out of hand," agreed the neighbor. "They're so sharp they'll cut themselves. Take that Demochkin now—he broke his father's arm for him. Too much learning, that's what it is."

Nikita listened, glancing at their faces, clearly wanting to take part in the conversation. But he was too busy with his tea and could only nod approvingly. He was drinking glass after glass, getting warmer and warmer and more and more comfortable. The talk went on for a long time about one thing only—the evils of dividing up a household. It was clearly not theoretical but a real question of division in this very house—a division demanded by the second son, sitting right there in gloomy silence. The topic was evidently a painful one, preoccupying all the family, but out of politeness they didn't discuss their private affairs in front of outsiders. In the end, though, the old man could bear it no longer and with tears in his voice started saying that he wouldn't allow anyone to divide anything while he was alive, that thank God they had a good home, and if it was broken up they'd all have to go out into the wide world as beggars.

"Just like the Matveyevs," said the neighbor. "They had a fine home, but they split it and now no one has anything."

"And that's what you want," said the old man to his son.

The son made no reply, and an uncomfortable silence fell. It was interrupted by Petrushka, who had already harnessed the mare and come back indoors, still smiling, a few minutes earlier.

"Pullson has a fable about that," he said. "A father gave his sons a broom of birch twigs to break. In one go they couldn't do it, but twig by twig it was easy. It's just the same here," he said with a broad grin. "I'm ready!" he added.

"If you're ready, we'll be off," said Vassili Andreyich. "But as far as division's concerned, grandfather, don't give in. You earned it; you're the master. Take it up with the village elder. He'll sort it out."

"But he pesters me so! He just won't let go," the old man kept saying tearfully. "There's no peace to be had—it's as though the devil's got into him."

Meanwhile Nikita finished his fifth glass of tea and still didn't upend it, laying it on its side in the hope they'd pour him a sixth. But there was no water left in the samovar, the women gave him nothing more, and Vassili Andreyich started getting dressed. There was nothing to be done. Nikita got up as well, put the lump of sugar he had nibbled from every side back into the bowl, wiped his face, damp with sweat, with the hem of his jacket, and went to put on his kaftan.

Once dressed, he sighed heavily, thanked his hosts, took his leave of them, and went out of the warm, bright living quarters into the dark, cold passageway, where a droning wind tore past, driving snow in through the trembling outer doors. From there, he went out into the black yard.

Petrushka was standing in his overcoat in the middle of the courtyard beside his mare, smiling and reciting a poem from Paulson. "Storms hides the heavens in darkness, spinning the snowflakes wild, ah it howls like an animal, ah it cries like a child."[14]

Nikita nodded his head approvingly, untangling the reins.

The old man came out with Vassili Andreyich, carrying a lantern into the passage to light his way. The wind put it out instantly. Even in the yard you could tell the blizzard was far fiercer than before.

"A tidy little breeze!" thought Vassili Andreyich. "I mayn't get there after all—but I have to go. Business is business. I'm all ready—and what's more, my host's harnessed his horse on my account. God willing, we'll get there all right."

The old man was also thinking they ought not to go, but he'd already tried to dissuade them and been ignored. No point in further persuasion. "Maybe age makes me overcautious, and they'll get there quite safely," he thought. "And at least we'll get to bed early, without extra bother."

Petrushka wasn't even thinking about danger, he knew the road and the surrounding countryside so well. Besides, the line about "spinning snowflakes wild" cheered him, it expressed so exactly what was happening out of doors.

As for Nikita, he didn't want to go at all, but long ago he'd got used to giving up his own wishes for the whims of the people he served.

So there was no one to stop them setting out on their journey.

5

Vassili Andreyich went up to the sledge, scarcely able to make out where it was in the darkness. He got in and took the reins.

"You go first!" he shouted.

Petrushka, kneeling in his low, wide sledge, let his horse go. Mukhorty had been neighing for some time. Scenting the mare in front of him, he started after her, and they drove out into the street. Once again they went through the outskirts by the familiar road, past the yard with its frozen washing on the line—quite invisible now. Past the threshing barn, almost completely snowed under, snow still pouring off its roof. Past the same dismally moaning, whistling, and tossing willows. Out they came into the snowy sea, raging above and below them. The wind was so strong when it hit them sideways the travelers leaned against it like yachtsmen. The sledge tilted, and the horse was shouldered to one side. Petrushka drove his mare at an easy trot, cheerfully shouting back to them. Mukhorty strained after the mare.

When they had driven on like that for about ten minutes, Petrushka turned around and shouted something to them. Neither Vassili Andreyich nor Nikita could hear for the wind, but they guessed they'd come to the turn. True enough, Petrushka turned to the right, the wind shifted from the side full into their faces again, and on their right something dark could be glimpsed through the snow. It was the little bush at the turning.

"Well, God be with you!"

"Thank you, Petrushka!"

"Storms hide the heavens in darkness!" Petrushka shouted, and vanished from sight.

"There's a poet for you," said Vassili Andreyich, and flicked the reins.

"Yes, a fine lad, a real good sort," said Nikita.

They drove on.

Nikita sat huddled in silence, his chin tucked in tight so his skimpy beard covered his neck, trying to conserve the warmth of his tea at the farm. In front of him the straight lines of the shafts constantly deceived him into thinking they were the verges of a beaten highway. He could see the horse's swaying haunches, its knotted tail swinging to one side, and ahead, the high yoke, Mukhorty's tossing head, neck, and streaming mane. Occasionally the roadside markers swam into view, reassuring him that, so far, they were keeping to the road and there was nothing for him to do.

Vassili Andreyich held the reins, leaving it to Mukhorty to choose his own way. But in spite of his rest in the village, Mukhorty ran reluctantly and seemed to be pulling to one side of the road, so that Vassili Andreyich had to correct him several times.

"That's one stake on the right, and there's another, and that's a third," Vassili Andreyich counted to himself. "And that's the forest ahead," he thought, looking at something dark ahead. But what he had taken for a forest was only a bush. They passed the bush, and went on for another twenty-five meters, but neither the forest nor the fourth stake appeared. "It must be the forest in a minute," thought Vassili Andreyich, and, invigorated by the vodka and the tea, cracked the reins. The good little horse obediently kept going—now at an amble, now at a slow trot—in the direction he was told, although he knew quite well that it was the wrong direction.

"We've gone and lost it again!" said Vassili Andreyich, pulling the horse up.

Without a word, Nikita got off the sledge, holding tight to his kaftan, which the wind kept plastering against him, then blowing wide, tearing it from his shoulders. He set off, plunging about in the snow again, first on one side, then the other. Three times he vanished from sight completely. At last he returned and took the reins from Vassili Andreyich.

"We need to go right," he said, sternly and decisively, turning the horse.

"Well, if you want to go right, then go right," said Vassili Andreyich, handing over the reins and pushing his frozen hands into his sleeves.

Nikita didn't reply.

"Come on, flower; make an effort," he shouted to the horse, but in spite of the shaken reins Mukhorty only went at an amble.

The snow was knee-deep in places. At every step, the sledge moved forward with a jerk.

Nikita got out the whip and hit him once. The good little horse, unused to the whip, leapt forward at a trot, but fell back into an amble and then a slow walk immediately. They went on for five minutes. It was so dark, and the smoking snow billowed so thick from above and below, that sometimes even the horse's tall yoke couldn't be seen. And sometimes, it seemed, the sledge stood still, while the field ran backward. Suddenly the horse stopped sharply, evidently sensing something wrong ahead. Dropping the reins, Nikita leapt lightly down once more and went in front of Mukhorty to see what had made him stop. Before he could take a single step forward his feet slipped from under him and he rolled down a steep incline.

"Whoa there!" he muttered as he fell, trying to resist, but he couldn't stop himself and came to a halt only when his legs shot into a deep snowdrift at the bottom of the gully.

A thick drift hanging over the edge of the hollow was disturbed by his fall and came down on him, filling his collar with snow.

"What a mean thing to do!" Nikita said reproachfully to the gully and the drift, shaking out the snow from his collar.

"Nikita! Hey, Nikit!" Vassili Andreyich shouted from above.

But Nikita didn't answer.

He was too busy. He shook himself down, then he hunted for the whip, which he'd lost rolling down the slope. Once he found the whip, he tried to climb straight back up where he came down, but there was no way up. He kept slipping backward, so he had to go along the bottom of the hollow to find another route. Six meters further on he managed, with difficulty, to climb up the drop on all fours, and went back along the top edge of the gully to where the horse should be. He couldn't make out either horse or sledge, but because he was walking into the wind, he heard the shouts of Vassili Andreyich, and the neighing of Mukhorty, before he saw either of them.

"I'm coming, I'm coming; what's all the fuss about?" he muttered.

It was only when he got right up to them that he saw the horse and sledge, and Vassili Andreyich standing by them, looking huge.

"Where the hell did you get to? We've got to go back. At least we can go back to Grishkino," Nikita's master began angrily.

"I'd happily go back, Vassili Andreyich, but which way should we go? There's such a drop here, once in you'd never get out. I whacked in so deep I could hardly get myself out again."

"But we can't stay here, can we? We have to drive somewhere," said Vassili Andreyich.

Nikita said nothing. He sat down in the sledge with his back to the wind, took off his felt boots, shook out the snow that had got into them, and, taking some straw, painstakingly stuffed it into the hole in his left boot from the inside.

Vassili Andreyich kept silent, as though leaving everything to Nikita. Having got his boots back on, Nikita swung his feet back into the sledge, put on his gloves again, took the reins, and turned the horse alongside the gully. But they hadn't gone more than a hundred steps before Mukhorty stopped again. The gully was in front of them once more.

Nikita got out again and went off yet again to plunge about in the snow. He walked around for some time. Finally he reappeared on the opposite side from where he had set out.

"Andreyich, are you alive?" he shouted.

"Over here!" Vassili Andreyich called back. "Now what?"

"I can't make anything out. It's dark. There are gullies of some kind. We'll have to drive back into the wind."

They drove on a bit. Nikita walked off again and plunged about in the snow again. He sat down again, plunged about again, and at last rested by the sledge, quite out of breath.

"Now what?" asked Vassili Andreyich.

"What d'you mean, what? I'm worn out, that's what. The horse has had enough, too."

"Then what are we to do?"

"Just wait a minute."

Nikita went off again but came back quickly.

"Keep behind me," he said, going in front of the horse.

Vassili Andreyich wasn't giving orders anymore, but obediently did what Nikita told him.

"This way, follow me!" Nikita shouted, going off quickly to the right, seizing Mukhorty's reins and leading him down into some snowdrift.

At first the horse resisted, then darted forward, hoping to jump the drift, but failed and landed in it up to his neck.

"Get out!" Nikita yelled at Vassili Andreyich, who was still sitting in the sledge, and, grasping one of the shafts he started moving the sledge up to the horse. "I know it's difficult, lovey," he said to Mukhorty, "but what can we do? Make a little effort. Come on, just a little one," he urged.

The horse jerked forward once, twice, but still couldn't get out of the drift. He sat back again, as if considering something.

"Come on, brother; that's not the way," said Nikita, reproaching Mukhorty. "Try again."

Once more Nikita pulled on his shaft and Vassili Andreyich did the same on the other side. The horse shook his head, then lunged forward.

"That's it, lovey, come on—you won't sink!" Nikita cried.

One plunge, another, a third, and the horse finally scrambled out of the drift. He stopped, breathing heavily and shaking himself.

Nikita wanted to lead him on, but Vassili Andreyich was so puffed in his two overcoats, he couldn't walk and tumbled into the sledge.

"Let me get my breath back," he said, untying the kerchief he had wound around the collar of his overcoat when they were in the village.

"You're all right, just lie there," said Nikita. "I'll lead him." And with Vassili Andreyich in the sledge he led the horse by the bridle—down ten paces, and then up a little, and then stopped.

The place where Nikita stopped was not right in a hollow, where the snow sweeping down its banks and collecting at the bottom would have buried them altogether. Nevertheless it was partially sheltered from the wind by the side of the gully. There were moments when the wind seemed to drop slightly, but they didn't last. As if to make up for the lulls, the storm swooped down ten times stronger, whirling and tearing at them even more cruelly. Such a gust struck them just when Vassili

Andreyich, having regained his breath, got out of the sledge and came up to Nikita to discuss what they should do next. Both instinctively bent over and waited to speak until the frenzy of the blast had died down. Mukhorty, too, laid back his ears discontentedly and shook his head. As soon as the squall had spent itself slightly, Nikita took off his gloves, tucked them into his belt, and began unfastening the straps of the shaft bow.

"What on earth are you doing?" asked Vassili Andreyich.

"Unhitching. What else can we do? I've no strength left," said Nikita, as though excusing himself.

"Can't we get out somewhere?"

"We can't get out anywhere, we'll just torment the horse. The poor thing's whacked as it is," said Nikita, pointing at the horse obediently standing there, ready and waiting, its wet, curved sides heaving. "We'll have to spend the night here," he repeated, just as though he was planning to spend the night at a coaching inn, and he started unbuckling the hame strap.[15]

The hames sprang apart.

"But won't we freeze?" said Vassili Andreyich.

"So? If we're to freeze, we can't refuse," said Nikita.

6

Vassili Andreyich was quite warm in his two fur coats, especially after his efforts in the snowdrift, but he felt a sudden chill run down his back when he realized they really would have to spend the night here. To calm himself, he sat down in the sledge and started getting out his cigarettes and matches.

Meanwhile, Nikita unharnessed the horse. He undid the girth and the back band, unhitched the reins, took off the tug, pulled out the high shaft bow, and kept up an encouraging conversation with the horse throughout.

"Come on, come on, step out of that," he said, leading Mukhorty out of the shafts. "Look, we'll tether you here. I'll put a bit of straw down and get your bridle off," he went on, doing as he said. "When you've had a bite you'll feel more cheerful."

But you could see that Mukhorty wasn't reassured by Nikita's words. He was anxious; he kept stepping from one hoof to the other, pressing up against the sledge, trying to turn his back to the wind, and rubbing his head against Nikita's sleeve.

As though not wanting to refuse the kind offer of straw Nikita pushed under his muzzle, Mukhorty nosed up a tuft from the sledge, but immediately decided this was no time for straw and dropped it. The wind instantly carried it away, scattered it, and covered it with snow.

"Now we'll make a signal," said Nikita, turning the sledge into the wind and, binding the shafts together with the back band, he raised them upright and pulled them up to the front of the sledge. "Now when we get snowed under, good folk will see the shafts and dig us out," said Nikita, slapping his gloves together and putting them back on. "That's what the old ones taught me."

Meanwhile, Vassili Andreyich had undone his fur coat and, holding its wide skirt against the wind, was striking one sulfur match after another on the steel box. But his hands were trembling. Match after match flared and went out, either before it had caught properly or just as he was bringing it up to the cigarette. At last one match burned well, momentarily lighting up the fur of his overcoat, his cupped hand with the gold signet ring on his forefinger, the oat straw poking out from under the sacking covered in snow—and the cigarette caught light. He inhaled greedily a couple of times, swallowed, and blew the smoke out through his mustache, but when he wanted to inhale again, the wind tore off the glowing tip of tobacco and scurried it away after the straw.

Even these few gulps of tobacco smoke cheered Vassili Andreyich.

"Well, that's it, then. We'll stop here for the night," he said decisively. "Hang on a minute, I'll make a flag as well," he added, picking up the kerchief which he'd unwound from his collar and dropped into the sledge. Taking his gloves off, he stood on the front of the sledge and, stretching up to reach the back band, tightly knotted the kerchief to it right by the shaft.

The kerchief instantly fluttered desperately, flinging itself against the shafts, convulsing, stretching, and flapping.

"Just look at that!" said Vassili Andreyich, admiring his handiwork and settling back into the sledge. "We'd be warmer together, but there isn't room for two," he added.

"I'll find myself somewhere," said Nikita, "but we must cover the horse, he's all of a sweat, poor thing. Forgive me," he added, and going up to the sledge, pulled the sacking out from under Vassili Andreyich.

Having got the sacking, he folded it in two. Undoing the loin strap and taking off the bellyband, he covered Mukhorty with it.

"It'll all keep you warmer, silly," he said, buckling on the bellyband and loin strap over the sacking. "Can you spare me that ticking? And give me a little bit of straw?" he said, finishing with the horse and going up to the sledge again.

Pulling out both things from under Vassili Andreyich, Nikita went to the back of the sledge, dug himself out a small hollow in the snow there, lined it with straw, pulled his cap low, wrapped his kaftan tight, covered himself with the ticking, and sat down in the straw he had strewn, leaning against the back of the sledge which sheltered him from the wind and snow.[16]

Vassili Andreyich shook his head at what Nikita was doing—in his habitual disapproval of peasant ignorance and stupidity—and began settling himself for the night.

He spread out the remaining straw more evenly in the sledge, arranging a thicker layer under his side, and, thrusting his hands deep in his sleeves, snuggled his head into the front corner of the sledge against the splashboard, which sheltered him from the wind.

He didn't want to sleep. He lay and thought—thought about the one and only thing, the single object, the sole reason, the joy and pride of his life. He thought about how much money he had made, and how much he could still make; he thought about how much other people he knew had made and how much money they had, and how these people made their money in the past and how they made it now, and how he, just like them, could still make a great deal more money. Buying the Goriachkin forest was immensely important to him. On this alone he hoped to make an immediate profit of some ten thousand rubles, perhaps. And he began totting up the value of the woodland he had inspected in the autumn, in which he had counted every single tree over a stretch of five acres.

"The oak will go for sledge runners. The logs—for building, obviously. And beside that there'll be thirty sazhen of firewood to each desyatina.[17] That means that at the very least there'll be two hundred and twenty-five rubles' worth left on every desyatina. Fifty-six desyatinas means fifty-six hundreds, and another fifty-six hundreds, and fifty-six tens, and another fifty-six tens, and then fifty-six fives. . . ." He saw that it came to more than twelve thousand rubles, but couldn't calculate it exactly without an abacus. "Still, I won't give ten thousand for it, only eight thousand, to allow a deduction for the clearings. I'll butter up the surveyor—a hundred, or a hundred and fifty, should do it, and he'll reckon up five desyatinas of clearings. And I'll get it for eight thousand. I'll give him three thousand cash down. That'll soften him up," he thought, squeezing his arm against the wallet in his pocket. "God knows how we lost our way after the turnoff! The forest should be here, and the watchman's hut. We should hear dogs barking. But of course they don't bark when you want them." He moved his collar away from his ear and started listening. There was nothing to be heard but the perpetual howling of the wind, the kerchief fluttering and smacking against the shafts, and the snow stinging the sledge's woodwork. He covered himself up again.

"If we'd only known, we'd have stayed the night. Well, it doesn't matter, we'll get there tomorrow. It's only one more day. The others won't set out in weather like this." And he remembered that on the ninth the butcher was meant to pay for the wethers. "He meant to come himself; he won't find me at home, and the wife won't know how to get the money out of him. She hasn't a clue, really uneducated. No idea how things should be done," he thought, remembering how awkward she had been with the district police officer who visited them for the festival the day before. "What d'you expect? She's a woman! What's she seen in her life? What sort of a household did we have when our parents were alive? It wasn't bad: a rich peasant's holding—an oat mill and a coaching inn, that was the whole property. And what have I achieved in fifteen years? A shop, two taverns, a mill, a grain store, two farms on lease, a house with an iron-roofed barn," he counted off with pride. "Not like in our parents' time! And whose name counts in the district? Brekhunov.

"And why's that? Because I keep my mind on the job, I put an effort into it, not like the others, layabouts and wastrels. I don't sleep at nights. Blizzard or no blizzard, I'm on the road. And so things get done. They think they can make money larking about. No, take pains and rack your brains! That's what gets you out in the fields at night, sleepless the whole night long. Your pillow spinning from the thoughts in your head," he reflected proudly. "They think you get to be somebody just by luck. Look at the Mironovs—they're millionaires now. And for why? Hard work. Man strives and God provides. God only grant me good health!"

And the thought that he could be a millionaire like Mironov, who had pulled himself up from nothing, excited Vassili Andreyich so much he felt the need to talk to somebody. But there was no one to talk to. If only he could have got to Goriachkin, he'd have talked to the landowner and shown him a thing or two.

"Good Lord, what a wind! It'll snow us in so deep we won't be able to get out in the morning!" he thought, listening to a gust of wind driving against the front of the sledge, bending the wood and thrashing it with snow. He lifted himself up and looked around. In the white wavering darkness he could only see Mukhorty's dark head and back, covered with the flapping sackcloth, and his thick, knotted tail. Around them, on every side, before and behind, there was the same monotonous whitely wavering darkness, sometimes appearing to lighten slightly, only to grow thicker still.

"I shouldn't have listened to Nikita," he thought. "We should have driven on; we would have come out somewhere or other. At least we could have gone back to Grishkino, and stayed the night with Taras. Now we've got to sit here all night. But what was it I was thinking? Yes, God helps those that help themselves—not the loafers, layabouts, and fools. I must have a smoke!" He sat up, took out his cigarette case, and lay down on his stomach, to shelter the match flame with the skirt of his greatcoat, but the wind found a way in and blew out one match after another. In the end he managed to light one and began smoking. The fact that he'd got his own way pleased him very much. Although the wind smoked more of the cigarette than he did, he still got a good two or three puffs, and felt more cheerful. He threw himself into the back of the sledge again, wrapped himself up, started reminiscing and daydreaming—and suddenly, quite unexpectedly, lost consciousness and fell asleep.

But suddenly it was as though something jolted him and woke him up. Whether it was Mukhorty snatching some straw from under him, or something inside him, he was wide awake, his heart beating so quickly and with such force, the sledge seemed to be shaking under him. He opened his eyes. Everything was unchanged around him, but it did seem lighter. "It's dawn," he thought. "It can't be long till morning." But he remembered at once that it was only getting lighter because the moon had risen. He propped himself up and looked first at the horse. Mukhorty was still standing with his back to the wind, shivering all over. One side of the snow-covered sacking had blown back, the loin strap had slipped sideways, and the snowy head with its waving fringe and mane could be seen more clearly. Vassili Andreyich bent over to the back of the sledge and peered over the side. Nikita was still sitting in his original position. His legs, and the ticking covering him, were thickly overlaid with snow. "I hope that peasant doesn't freeze; his clothes aren't too good. I'll be answerable for him, too. What a shiftless lot they are! Pure peasant ignorance, of course," thought Vassili Andreyich. He would have taken the sacking off the horse to cover Nikita, but it was too cold to get up and move about, and he was afraid the horse might freeze. "And what made me take him? It was all her stupidity!" Vassili Andreyich thought, remembering his unloved wife, and rolled back into his former place in the front of the sledge. "My uncle once sat out a whole night in the snow like this," he remembered, "and nothing happened. Yes, but when Sebastian was dug out," he went on, promptly remembering another case, "he was dead, stiff all over, a frozen carcass.

"If I'd stayed the night at Grishkino, none of this would have happened." And, painstakingly wrapping himself tighter so that the heat of the fur didn't get lost at any point but warmed him everywhere—at his neck, his knees, and the soles of his feet—he shut his eyes and tried to go to sleep again. But now, however hard he tried, he couldn't drop off again. On the contrary, he felt completely wakeful and alert. Once more he began reckoning his profits, the debts owing to him. Once again, he began bragging to himself and gloating over his status, but now everything kept getting interrupted by a creeping terror and the nagging question, why hadn't he stayed the night in Grishkino? "That would have been something, lying warm on a bunk." He turned over several times, tucked himself in, tried to find a more comfortable position that was better sheltered from the wind, but everything seemed wrong to him. He kept lifting himself up, changing his place, bundling up his legs, shutting his eyes, and falling still again. But either his legs in their tight-fitting felt boots started aching, or a draft worked its way in somewhere, and having lain still a little while, the irksome thought would come back to him—how he could now be lying peacefully in the warm house at Grishkino—and he would sit up again, turn around, wrap himself up, and try to settle down again.

Once it seemed to Vassili Andreyich that he could hear cocks crowing in the distance. He felt glad, turned back his greatcoat, and started listening intently, but however hard he strained to hear, there wasn't a sound, except the wind whining in the shafts and slapping the kerchief, and the snow pelting against the sides of the sledge.

Nikita was still sitting just as he had first sat down that night, not shifting at all, and not even answering Vassili Andreyich, who appealed to him several times. "What does he care? He must be asleep," Vassili Andreyich thought resentfully, peering over the back of the sledge at Nikita under his thick covering of snow.

Vassili Andreyich sat up and lay down again twenty times or more. He felt as though this night would never end. "It must be near dawn by now," he thought once, sitting up and looking around. "I'll just have a look at my watch. It'll be chilly unbuttoning. But if it's coming up for morning, things'll cheer up a bit. We can start harnessing." In the depths of his soul Vassili Andreyich knew perfectly well it couldn't be morning yet, but he was getting more and more afraid. He wanted to know the time, and to deceive himself about the time. He carefully undid the hooks of his sheepskin and plunged his hand into his breast, rummaging about for a long time before he could find his waistcoat. With considerable effort he dragged out his silver watch with its enamel flowers and peered at it. You could see nothing without a light. Once again he turned face downward on his hands and knees as he had done when he was smoking, got out his matches, and set about lighting them. This time he was more efficient, feeling with his fingertips for the match with the fattest phosphorus head, and lit it at the first attempt. He brought the watch face under the light, glanced at it, and couldn't believe his eyes.... It was ten past midnight. The whole night still lay ahead of him.

"Oh what a long night this is!" thought Vassili Andreyich. A chill ran down his back. Hooking up his sheepskin and wrapping up again, he huddled into the corner of the sledge, preparing to wait patiently. Suddenly, through the uniform tumult of the wind he heard a new and living sound. It grew steadily louder and, at its clearest, just as steadily died away. There was no doubt that it was a wolf. And this wolf was so close that you could clearly hear on the wind the tone of his cry changing as he shifted his jaws. Vassili Andreyich turned back his collar and listened attentively. Mukhorty was listening equally tensely, turning his ears, and when the wolf stopped keening he shifted his legs and gave a warning snort. After that Vassili Andreyich certainly couldn't get to sleep again, nor even calm himself. The more he tried to think of his enterprises and profits, his reputation, his wealth and his worth, the more fear possessed him, and all his thoughts were suffused by one thought—why hadn't he stayed the night at Grishkino?

"Who cares about the forest? I've business enough as it is, thank God. Oh, I wish the night would end!" he said to himself. "They say drunks freeze to death," he thought, "and I've had a drink or two." And scrutinizing his sensations, he felt that he was beginning to tremble, not knowing what he was trembling from, cold or fear. He kept trying to wrap himself up and lie as before, but couldn't anymore. He couldn't stay still; he wanted to get up and busy himself with something, to choke back the fear rising in him, against which he felt quite powerless. He took out his matches and cigarettes again, but there were only three matches left, all of them bad. All three were duds and failed to catch.

"Devil take it! God rot you!" he swore, cursing he knew not what, and threw the crushed cigarette away. He wanted to chuck away the box, too, but stopped himself and thrust it into his pocket. He became so restless, he couldn't stay still any longer. He got out of the sledge and, standing with his back to the wind, started tightening his belt low on his hips again.

"What's the point of lying there, waiting for death to come? To get on horseback and ride off, now——" it suddenly occurred to him. "The horse won't stop if I'm on its back. As for him," he thought, of Nikita, "he's going to die anyway. What sort of a life has he got? Even his life hardly matters to him—but as for me, thank God, I've got something to live for...."

And, unhitching the horse, he threw the reins over Mukhorty's neck and tried to leap on, but his two overcoats and his boots were so heavy he slipped off. Then he got up on the sledge and tried to mount from that. But the sledge rocked under his weight, and he slid off again. Finally, at the third attempt, he brought the horse closer to the sledge and, carefully standing on one side, managed to get himself belly down across the horse's back. Having lain like that for a little, he shoved himself forward once, twice, and finally swung his leg over the horse's back and seated himself, digging his soles down lengthwise along the breeching strap. The jolt of the rocking sledge woke Nikita, who raised himself up and appeared to Vassili Andreyich to be saying something.

"Listen to you idiots! What, am I going to die like that, just for nothing?" Vassili Andreyich shouted, and, tucking the loose skirts of his fur coat under his knees, he turned the horse and drove him away from the sledge, in the direction where he thought the forest and the watchman's hut ought to be.

7

Ever since Nikita had sat down behind the back of the sledge, covered in the ticking, he had stayed absolutely still. Like all people who live with nature and know want, he was patient and could wait calmly for hours and even days, feeling neither anxiety nor irritation. He heard his master calling him, but didn't answer because he didn't want to move or to answer. Although he was still warm from the tea he had drunk and from moving about a lot, clambering through the snowdrifts, he knew his warmth wouldn't last long. He had no strength left to get warmer by moving about. He felt as tired as a horse feels when it stops dead and however hard it's hit, can't go any farther, and the master sees the horse must be fed before it can work again. One foot in the torn boot had already gone numb and he couldn't feel his big toe anymore. Apart from that, his whole body was getting colder and colder. The thought came to him that he might, and very probably would, die that night, but this thought didn't seem particularly unpleasant to him, nor particularly frightening. It didn't seem particularly unpleasant because his whole life hadn't been a perpetual holiday but, on the contrary, an uninterrupted round of hard labor, which was beginning to tire him. Nor was it particularly frightening because, apart from the masters like Vassili Andreyich that he served here, in this life, he always felt himself dependent on the main master, the one who sent him into life. And he knew that even in death he would stay in this master's power, and wouldn't be treated badly. "Am I sorry to abandon the old things, the ones I know, where I feel at home? Well, nothing to be done, I'll have to get used to the new."

"Sins?" he thought, and remembered his drunkenness, the money he had squandered on drink, his ill-treatment of his wife, the swearing, the church days missed, the neglected fasts, and all the things the priest rebuked him for at confession. "They're certainly sins. But did I bring them down on myself? God must have made me that way. So, they're sins. And so what?"

And he thought first about what might happen to him that night, and then, no longer reverting to that, he gave himself up to the memories that came of their own accord. He thought first of Marfa's arrival two days before, and the workers' drunkenness, and his own renunciation of alcohol, and then of this day's journey, and the home of Taras, and the talk of division; and then he thought of his son, and of Mukhorty, who would get warm now under the sacking, and then of his master, who was making the sledge squeak as he turned around in it. "He can't be glad he came, either, poor soul," he thought. "You wouldn't want to die with a life like that. Not like me." And all these ideas began plaiting themselves together, mixing in his head, and he fell asleep.

But when Vassili Andreyich rocked the sledge mounting the horse, and the backboard Nikita was leaning against jerked away completely and then hit him in the spine with one of the runners, he woke up and, willy-nilly, had to change his position. Straightening out his legs with difficulty and shaking the snow off them, he got up, and a piercing chill instantly ran through him. When he saw what was going on, he wanted Vassili Andreyich to leave him the sacking, which the horse no longer needed, so that he could cover himself with it. That was what he shouted to Vassili Andreyich.

But Vassili Andreyich didn't stop and vanished into the snowy dust.

Left on his own, Nikita thought for a moment what he should do. He felt far too weak to go looking for houses. He couldn't sit down anymore where he had sat earlier—the place was all covered in snow. Even in the sledge, he felt he wouldn't get warm because he had nothing to cover himself and he was no longer remotely warmed by his kaftan and sheepskin. He felt as cold as if he were only wearing a shirt. He became frightened. "God in Heaven!" he muttered, and the knowledge that he wasn't alone, that someone heard him and wouldn't abandon him, calmed him. He took a deep breath and, without taking the ticking off his head, got into the sledge and lay down in his master's place.

But it was quite impossible to get warm in the sledge either. At first his whole body trembled, then the trembling passed off and he gradually began to lose consciousness. Whether he was dying, or falling asleep, he couldn't tell, but he felt equally prepared for both.[18]

8

Meanwhile Vassili Andreyich urged Mukhorty on with his heels and the ends of the reins, in the direction where for some reason he assumed the forest and watchman's hut should be. The snow was blinding him, and the wind seemed to want to stop him, but he leaned forward, constantly pulling his fur coat close and tucking it between himself and the cold bellyband that prevented him getting a proper grip, whipping Mukhorty on without respite. Obediently but with difficulty, the horse went at an amble where he was told.

For about five minutes Vassili Andreyich rode in what seemed to him a straight line, seeing nothing except the horse's head and the white waste, and hearing nothing except the wind tearing past the horse's ears and the collar of his fur coat.

Suddenly something darkened in front of him. His heart leapt, and he rode toward the blackness, already seeing in it the walls of village houses. But the black thing wasn't stationary, it kept moving; and it wasn't a village, but some tall wormwood stalks, sticking up through the snow in the rough ground between two fields, desperately tossing about under a wind that dashed them sideways, hissing through them. And for some reason the sight of these weeds, mercilessly tormented by the wind, made Vassili Andreyich shudder; and he hurriedly began beating the horse on, not noticing that when he rode up to the clump of worm-wood he had changed tack completely, and was now urging the horse in the opposite direction from before, still imagining that he was riding toward the place where the watchman's hut should be. But the horse kept pulling to the right, and so he kept pulling it to the left.

Something grew dark in front of him again. He felt glad, sure that this time it really must be the village. But it was just another bit of scrub. For some reason the dreadful shaking of the tall, dry weeds filled Vassili Andreyich with terror. It wasn't just that it was a very sim-ilar clump of wormwood. There were hoof prints beside it, drifting over with snow. Vassili Andreyich stopped, leaned over, and glanced at them. It was a horse track, lightly dusted with snow. There was no doubt it could only be his own. He was going round in a circle, and not a wide one either. "I'll perish like this!" he thought, and to ward off his terror, he beat the horse on even more fiercely, peering into the white snowy gloom, in which little dots of light seemed to him to be sparkling, only to vanish when he looked at them. Once he thought he heard dogs barking, or wolves howling, but the sounds were so faint and indistinct, he couldn't be sure whether he had actually heard something or only imagined it. He stopped, and started listening intently.

Suddenly a fearful, deafening cry broke out right beside him, and everything shuddered and trembled under him. Vassili Andreyich grabbed the horse's neck, but the horse's neck was all shaking, too, and the terrible cry became even more horrifying. For some seconds Vassili Andreyich couldn't come to himself or understand what was happening. But it was only Mukhorty, neighing in his loud, resonant voice, either trying to cheer himself or calling for help. "Bloody brute! You terrified the life out of me, damn you!" Vassili Andreyich said to himself. But even when he understood the reason for his terror, he couldn't shake it off.

"I must stop and think. I must calm down," he kept saying to himself, and at the same time couldn't stop himself beating the horse on, not noticing that now they were going with the wind rather than against it. His body was frozen and painful, especially his thighs, which were unprotected and rubbed against the brass-studded bellyband; his feet and hands trembled, and his breathing came in great jerks.

He can see himself perishing in this dreadful snowy waste. He sees nothing that can save him.

Suddenly the horse gave way under him. It was caught in a snowdrift, thrashing about and keeling over sideways. Vassili Andreyich tumbled off, yanking the breeching strap which had supported his leg, and pulling to one side the bellyband he had been holding on to. The minute Vassili Andreyich was off his back, the horse righted himself, strained, lunged, and leapt. Neighing again, dragging the flapping sacking and bellyband behind him, he vanished from sight, leaving Vassili Andreyich alone in the snowdrift. Vassili Andreyich flung himself after him, but the snow was so deep, and his fur coats were so heavy, he sank in up to his knees at every step. After twenty steps at the most, he stopped, breathless. "The forest, the sheep, the leaseholds, the shop, the taverns, the house and barn and their iron roofs, my heir," he thought, "—what will become of them all? How can this be? It can't be—" flashed through his mind, and for some reason he remembered the wormwood he had twice ridden past, thrashing in the wind, and such horror came over him, he couldn't believe what was happening to him was real. "Isn't this all a dream?" he thought, and wanted to wake up, but there was no way of waking. This was real snow, stinging his face, covering him, and chilling his right hand, whose glove he had lost. And this was a real waste, the waste he was left in, lonely as that clump of weeds—to wait for certain, swift, and meaningless death.

"Queen of Heaven, holy father Nikolai, teacher of temperance!" he cried. And he remembered the prayers of the day before, the icon with its blackened face and gold leaf, and the candles he sold to be burned before the icon, which were brought back to him immediately afterward, and put back in their chest barely singed.[19] He began imploring the same Nicholas the Miracle Worker to save him, promising him prayers and candles. But at this very moment he understood, clearly and without question, that the dark face, the gold leaf, the candles, the priest, and the prayers—they were all very important and necessary there, in the church, but here they could do nothing for him. There was no connection, and could be no connection, between those candles and prayers and his present catastrophic situation.

"I mustn't lose heart," he thought. "I must follow the horse's tracks, and before they're covered over, too. He'll lead me out, or I might catch him. But I mustn't hurry, or I'll make matters worse." Yet in spite of his determination to go slowly, he threw himself forward at a run, falling constantly, heaving himself up, and falling again. The horse's tracks were already barely visible in the places where the snow wasn't deep. "I'm done for," thought Vassili Andreyich. "I'll lose track of him, and never catch up with him." But at that moment, glancing in front of him, he saw something dark. It was Mukhorty. And not only Mukhorty, but the sledge, its shafts and the kerchief. Mukhorty, with bellyband and sacking askew, was now standing not in his original place, but closer to the shafts, shaking his head, which was dragged down by the reins caught under his hooves. Vassili Andreyich had plunged into the same drift where he got stuck with Nikita. The horse had been bringing him back to the sledge, and he had leapt off him not more than fifty paces away.

9

Stumbling up to the sledge, Vassili Andreyich caught hold of it and stood still for a long time, trying to calm down and get his breath back. Nikita wasn't in his old place, and in the sledge something was lying covered up with snow. Vassili Andreyich guessed it was Nikita. Now his terror passed completely, and if he was afraid of anything, it was the horrible sensation of terror he had experienced on horseback—and especially when he was left on his own in the snowdrift. Whatever happened he had to ward off this terror, and to keep it at bay he had to do something, to busy himself in some way. And so the first thing he did was to put his back to the wind and undo his fur coat. Then, when he had got his breath back slightly, he shook the snow out of his boots and his left glove—the right one was hopelessly lost and probably completely snowed under by now. Then he did up his belt again, tight and low on the hips, as he used to do when he came out of his shop to buy grain the peasants brought on their carts. He got down to business. The first thing that occurred to him was to free the horse's legs. Vassili Andreyich did so, and, having untangled the rein, tethered Mukhorty to the iron staple on the front of the sledge, where he had been before. He was just about to go round the horse to put the loin strap, bellyband and sacking to rights, when he saw something moving in the sledge. Nikita's head poked out of the snow that had covered it completely. Half-frozen, he laboriously heaved himself into a sitting position, flapping his hand in front of his nose in the oddest way, just as though he was waving off flies. He went on flapping his hand and saying something, and it seemed to Vassili Andreyich that he was calling him. Vassili Andreyich left the sacking hanging crooked and came up to the sledge.

"What is it?" he asked. "What are you saying?"

"I—I'm d-dying, that's what," Nikita said, stumbling painfully. "Give what's owing to my boy or the old lady, it doesn't matter which."

"What, are you frozen?" asked Vassili Andreyich.

"I can feel ... I'm dying ... forgive me, for Christ's sake," said Nikita tearfully, still flapping his hand just as though shooing off flies.

Vassili Andreyich stood in silence, without moving, for half a minute and then suddenly, with the same decisiveness with which he shook hands over a good bargain, took a step back, pushed up his sleeves, and with both hands started shoveling the snow off Nikita and out of the sledge. When he'd shifted it all, he hastily undid his belt, opened his fur coat wide, and, pushing Nikita down, lay on top of him, covering him not only with his fur coat but his own glowing, overheated body. Pushing down the laps of his overcoat between the sledge sides and Nikita with his hands, and pinning the hem down with his knees, Vassili Andreyich lay prone, leaning his head on the front of the sledge. Now he heard neither the horse's movements, nor the howling wind, attending only to Nikita's breathing. At first Nikita lay motionless for a long time. Then he breathed in noisily and stirred.

"There you go! And you said you were dying. Lie there, get warm, and that's how we'll..." Vassili Andreyich began.

But to his great astonishment he could say no more, because tears came into his eyes and his lower jaw was trembling. He stopped speaking, and tried to swallow the thing rising in his throat. "That fright must have taken all the strength out of me," he thought. But his present weakness was not only not unpleasant, it gave him a particular gladness he had never felt before.

"And so we'll..." he repeated to himself, feeling a special, solemn tenderness. For quite a long time he lay like that in silence, wiping his eyes on the fur of his coat and tucking in its right corner, which the wind kept tugging loose, under his knee.

But he passionately wanted to tell someone how happy he was.

"Nikita!" he said.

"It's good, it's warm," came the answer from under him.

"That's it, brother. I would have died, too. You would have frozen, and I would..."

But his jaw shook again, his eyes filled with tears, and he couldn't go on.

"Well, never mind," he thought. "I know what I know."

And he fell silent. He lay still for a long time.

He was warmed underneath by Nikita, and warm on top from his greatcoats. Only his hands, holding the fur down at Nikita's sides, and his legs, constantly uncovered by the wind pulling his coattails loose, began to go numb. His right hand, without its glove, was coldest of all. But he wasn't thinking about his legs or his hands; he thought only about how he could warm the peasant lying under him.

Several times he glanced at the horse, and saw that his back was bare and that the bellyband and sacking were dangling in the snow, but he couldn't bring himself to leave Nikita for a minute, or disrupt his own sense of happiness. He was no longer in the least afraid.

"We'll get out of it this time, no fear!" he said to himself, meaning he'd get his peasant warm, and speaking with the same boastfulness he habitually used when talking of his purchases and sales.

Vassili Andreyich lay like that for one hour, and two, and three, without noticing how the time passed. At first his mind's eye was filled with impressions of the blizzard, the shafts, and the horse under its yoke, and memories of Nikita lying under him. Then they mingled with memories of the festival, his wife, the district police officer, the chest of candles, and Nikita again, lying under the chest. Then came peasants, buying and selling, and white walls, and houses roofed in iron, under which Nikita was lying. Then everything muddled together, one thing running into another and, like the colors of the rainbow fusing into a single white light, all his different perceptions ran into a single nothingness, and he fell asleep. He slept dreamlessly for a long time. Just before dawn, the dreams returned. He seemed to be standing before the chest of candles, and Tikhonov's widow was demanding a five-kopek candle for the holy day.

He tries to take a candle and give it to her, but his hands won't move, they are stuck in his pockets. He wants to come around the chest, but his legs won't move; his new, clean galoshes have grown into the stone floor, and he can't lift them or get out of them. And suddenly the candle chest turns from a chest of candles into a bed; and Vassili Andreyich sees himself lying belly down on the candle chest, or rather his bed, in his house. And he is lying on his bed and can't get up, but he needs to get up, because in a minute Ivan Matveyich, the district police officer, is coming for him, and he must go with Ivan Matveyich, either to buy the forest or to put right Mukhorty's bellyband. And he asks his wife, "Mikolavna, hasn't he come?" and she says, "No, he hasn't come." And he hears someone driving up to the front steps. It must be him. No, they've gone past. "Mikolavna, Mikolavna, hasn't he come yet?" "Not yet." And he lies on his bed, and he still can't get up, and keeps waiting, and this waiting is dreadful and wonderful at the same time. And suddenly his joy is accomplished; the one he was waiting for has come, and it is no longer Ivan Matveyich, the district police officer, but someone else, the very one he was waiting for. He has come and is calling him, and this one, the one who is calling him, is the one who called him and told him to lie on Nikita. And Vassili Andreyich is glad that this one has come for him. "I'm coming!" he cries joyfully, and his cry wakes him. He is awake, but he is utterly different from who he was when he fell asleep. He tries to rise, and he cannot; he tries to move his hand, and cannot; his foot, and cannot. He tries to turn his head, but this he cannot do. And he is surprised, but not in the least disturbed. He understands that this is death, but this doesn't trouble him either. He remembers that Nikita is lying under him, that he was warmed and is alive, and it seems to him that he is Nikita and Nikita is he, and that his life is not in himself, but in Nikita. He strains his ears, and hears breathing, and even a light snore, from Nikita. "Nikita is alive, and that means I am living too," he says to himself triumphantly.

And he remembers his money, his shop, his house, his buying and selling, and the Mironov millions, and it is hard for him to understand why that man, whom people called Vassili Brekhunov, troubled himself with all those things that troubled him. "Oh well, he didn't know what it was all about," he thinks, of Vassili Brekhunov. "He didn't know, as now I know, and know for sure. Now I know." And again he hears the one who called, calling him. "I'm coming, I'm coming!" his whole being replies in joy and tenderness. And he feels he is free and nothing more can hold him.

And Vassili Andreyich saw nothing more, heard nothing more, felt nothing more in this world.

The snow smoked on around them. The spinning snowflakes wildly covered the furs of the dead Vassili Andreyich, Mukhorty shuddering in every limb, the barely visible sledge, and Nikita, lying in its depths, warm under his dead master.

10

Nikita woke before dawn. An eddy of cold down his back woke him. He was dreaming that as he was driving home from the mill with flour belonging to his master, he missed the bridge crossing the stream and jammed the cart. And he sees that he climbed under the cart and heaved it up, straightening his back. But—a strange thing!—the cart doesn't move and sticks to his back, and he can neither shift it nor get out from under it. It has crushed the small of his back entirely. And how cold he is! It's obvious he has to get himself out. "Give over!" he says to whoever it is who's crushing his back with the cart. "Get the sacks off!" But the cart is getting colder and colder as it presses down on him, and suddenly something knocks sharply, and he wakes up completely and remembers everything. The cold cart is his dead, frozen master, lying on top of him. And Mukhorty is the one who knocked, hitting his hoof against the sledge a couple of times.

"Andreyich! Hey, Andreyich!" Nikita carefully calls his master, already guessing the truth and trying to straighten his back.

But Andreyich doesn't answer, and his belly and legs are as solid, cold, and heavy as iron weights.

"He must have died. Heaven be with him!" Nikita thinks.

He turns his head, clears away the snow in front of him with his hand, and opens his eyes. It is light; the same wind is humming in the shafts, the same snow is pouring down, with only this difference, that instead of lashing against the sides of the sledge, it is silently burying horse and sledge deeper and deeper, and not a movement or breath from the horse can be heard anymore. "He must have frozen to death, too," thinks Nikita. And indeed the hooves knocking against the sledge that woke Nikita were the frozen Mukhorty's death throes, his last attempt to keep on his feet.

"O God, O heavenly father, you must be calling me too," Nikita says to himself. "Thy will be done. But it is hard. Oh well, you can't die twice, and you can't avoid dying once. Only let it come quickly..." And he hides his hands again, shutting his eyes, and loses consciousness, quite convinced that now he is well and truly dying.

It wasn't till noon that day that peasants with spades dug out Vassili Andreyich and Nikita, just five hundred meters from the road and a kilometer from the village.

The snow had completely covered the sledge, but the shafts and kerchief above it could still be seen. Mukhorty stood up to his belly in snow, his tackle and sacking falling off his back. He was quite white. His dead head was pressed close against his stony throat. His nostrils had frozen over with icicles; his eyes were frosted over as if with tears. In one night he had grown so thin, nothing seemed left of him but skin and bone. Vassili Andreyich had hardened into a frozen carcass, his legs spread wide. So they dragged him, straddled as he was, off Nikita. His bulging, hawk-like eyes were frozen, and his open mouth under his clipped mustache was filled with snow.

Nikita was still alive, though freezing. When they woke him, he was sure he had died and what was happening to him now was not going on in this world but the next. The shouts of the peasants, digging him out and tumbling the dead body of Vassili Andreyich off him, surprised him at first. Did peasants in the other world have the same bodies as here and shout the same things? When he understood he was still here, in our world, he was more disappointed than pleased, especially when he realized that the toes of both his feet were frostbitten.

Nikita lay in hospital over two months. Three toes were amputated, but the rest healed, so he could go on working. He lived for another twenty years—first as a laborer, and then, in old age, as a watchman. He only died this year, at home with an icon at his head and a lit wax candle in his hands. Before his death he asked forgiveness of his old lady, and forgave her for the cooper. He said good-bye to his son and his grandchildren, and died, genuinely glad that his death freed his son and daughter-in-law from another mouth to feed. He was glad, too, that he was leaving this life, of which he was heartily tired, for that other life, which, with every year and every hour, had become more and more comprehensible and desirable to him.

NOTES

THE DEATH OF IVAN ILYICH

1. *eight hundred rubles:* In 1886, when this story was written, one ruble was worth the equivalent of about one dollar now. However, since incomes were considerably smaller at that time, such a raise would have been a proportionately larger percentage increase than today.
2. *law school:* The Imperial School of Jurisprudence was founded in Petersburg in 1835 as a private school where members of the hereditary nobility trained for legal and administrative careers.
3. *deacon:* literally, a church reader; a lay member who combined the functions of clerk, chorister, and reader.
4. *impure look:* Judging by the account given in Tolstoy's autobiographical *A Confession,* he is thinking of the awakened sexuality of adolescence.
5. *Privy Councillor:* third in the Table of Ranks established by Peter the Great in 1722. Holders of the top four grades were entitled to hereditary nobility.
6. *le phénix de la famille:* (French) "the family phoenix," or pride of the family.
7. *Scharmer's . . . respice finem . . . Donon's:* Scharmer was a fashionable tailor, and Donon's was a high-class restaurant, in Petersburg. The conventional Latin tag on Ivan Ilyich's watch chain will acquire ironic resonance. It means "Consider your end."
8. *Old Believers:* schismatics or dissenters of various sects, who rejected Patriarch Nikon's reforms in the mid-seventeenth century.
9. *bon enfant:* (French) "a good boy."

10. *il faut que jeunesse se passe:* (French) "Youth must have its fling."

11. *examining magistrate:* In 1860 the preliminary investigation of criminal cases was transferred from the police to the new, legal post of examining magistrate.

12. *comme il faut:* (French) "as it should be," proper.

13. *reformed Code of 1864:* The serfs were emancipated in 1861. This major reform was followed by the new judicial code of November 20, 1864. The judiciary was made independent of the administration. Chambers of Justice were set up in several large towns. A jury system was introduced. The new post of Justice of the Peace was created to deal with minor cases. Court proceedings were made public, with the litigants and their representatives in attendance and able to make oral representations. Previously, court proceedings had been conducted in camera, in the absence of the defendant and other interested parties, and with all material presented in written form (thus excluding the majority of Russia's population, which was illiterate).

14. *de gaîté de cœur:* (French) out of sheer willfulness.

15. *His oldest daughter was already sixteen:* A trivial error. Editors point out contradictions in Tolstoy's chronology. She should be ten—but Tolstoy overlooked six years, from 1874 to 1880.

16. *seventeen years:* The same error. Tolstoy has accounted for only eleven years of Ivan Ilyich's married life.

17. *Empress Maria's institutions:* charitable institutions and schools for young gentlewomen, founded by the dowager empress Maria Feodorovna in the reign of Tsar Alexander I.

18. *Apart from its importance for Russia, the predicted reshuffle:* Tolstoyan irony. Piotr Ivanovich, Ivan Simyonovich, Piotr Petrovich, and Zakhar Ivanovich—as their names suggest—are all nobodies jostling on the stairs of promotion and demotion.

19. *his sister and her husband:* commonly and erroneously corrected to Ivan Ilyich's brother-in-law (Praskovya Feodorovna's brother) and his wife, with whom they were staying in the country. But the Russian text states specifically Ivan Ilyich's sister and her husband. She and her husband, Baron Greff, another civil servant, lived in Petersburg (see p. 11) and were presumably inviting Ivan Ilyich to join them without his family while he settled into his prestigious new post.

20. *étagère:* a decorative set of shelves for knickknacks, a whatnot.

21. *Pasha and Lizanka:* Ivan Ilyich's softened good humor is evident in his use of diminutives for his wife, Praskovya, and daughter, Elizaveta.

22. *"Bear My Burden":* a charitable society patronized by the Empress.

23. *vint:* A variety of whist, *vint,* or Siberian whist, was introduced in Russia in 1870 and became very popular. It was normally played by a party of four. More players had to take turns sitting out.

24. *floating kidney, chronic catarrh, or a disease of the blind gut:* Floating kidney and chronic catarrh—modish diagnoses of the time—are both nonsensical, as Tolstoy was well aware. He uses these faintly absurd medical terms with a strong tone of irony. A disease of the blind gut is what we would now call appendicitis.

25. *he forgets the trumps:* So does Tolstoy. He has forgotten that Ivan Ilyich's partner declared "No trumps."

26. *Jean:* French for Ivan. It was an affected refinement among upper-class women to substitute French for Russian names.

27. *Kiesewetter's logic:* J. G. Kiesewetter (1766–1819) published a textbook of logic widely used in Russian schools, in a Russian translation.

28. *Vanya ... Mitya and Volodya ... Katenka:* Diminutives for "Ivan" as a child; his brothers, Dmitri and Vladimir, and his sister, Ekaterina.

29. *établissement:* Fancy French for "arrangement."

30. *rubakha:* the traditional high-collared Russian peasant shirt.

31. *Vassili Ivanovich ... has gone ... Praskovya Feodorovna gave orders:* In the Russian, Piotr uses the third person plural for both verbs—a servant's courtesy to the gentry he serves, in strong contrast to the intimate tone that has developed between Ivan Ilyich and Gerasim. Tolstoy has forgotten that on page 9 he called Ivan Ilyich's son Volodya (diminutive of Vladimir). Later he gets Petrishev's patronymic wrong.

32. *Sarah Bernhardt:* Sarah Bernhardt (1844–1923), the famous French actress, toured Russia during the winter of 1881–82.

33. *à la Capoul:* Hair parted down the middle with two curls falling on either side of the forehead—a style named after the French tenor Victor Capoul (1839–1924).

34. *Adrienne Lecouvreur:* An eighteenth-century actress whose life was dramatized in a play of 1849, written by A. E. Scribe and E. G. Legouvé. The lead was one of Sarah Bernhardt's most celebrated roles.

35. *it's time to go:* Tolstoy's italics. In this context, "glancing at her watch, a gift from her father" evokes Ivan Ilyich's own watch and medallion, with the motto "*respice finem.*" Liza is as incapable of foreseeing her own end as her father was—even with her father dying in front of her.

36. *The court is in session! ... the judge is coming:* Tolstoy is turning a pun the translation cannot reproduce exactly. In Russian "*sud idyot,*" the usher's cry,

means "the court is in session." But *sud* also means "trial," "judges," "bench," "judgment," "verdict." Tolstoy then twice repeats the usher's phrase, but reverses it to "*idyot sud*" so implying in fluid progression that the court is in session; the judge is coming; judgment is coming.

37. *nyanya:* nurse, nanny.

38. "*not the right thing*": In the Russian, *ne to* literally means "not it." The phrase spans a range of tones, from what is socially improper to what is morally wrong. Throughout the next two paragraphs Tolstoy repeats the same phrase, to mark Ivan Ilyich's gradual realization that what he thought socially acceptable was morally wrong. The done thing is not the right thing.

MASTER AND MAN

1. *the seventies ... the winter festival of St. Nicholas:* 1870s; now December 19 (New Style).

2. *merchant of the Second Guild:* Merchants were classed in guilds, according to their trade and size of capital.

3. *ten thousand rubles:* For a modern equivalent, see note 1 to "The Death of Ivan Ilyich." Later, Tolstoy changes its value. See note 17 below.

4. *added to them two thousand three hundred rubles from the church funds:* hardly honest practice on Vassili Andreyich's part.

5. *Mukhorty:* literally, the term for a bay horse dappled with gold.

6. *Women! There's no contradicting them!:* Literally, "She sticks to you like a wet leaf in the bathhouse" (in a sauna Russians used to beat themselves with birch twigs).

7. *Felt-soled* valenki: *Valenki* are felt boots—normal Russian winter wear in those days, and very good in dry snow, but not wet conditions. Tolstoy distinguishes between Vassili Andreyich's felt boots, which are covered with leather at the bottom, to protect against the wet, and Nikita's, which are not, just as he later distinguishes between the master's two fur-lined greatcoats and Nikita's torn sheepskin jacket and thin kaftan. See also note 16.

8. *Brekhunov never cheated anyone:* Vassili Andreyich is speaking of himself in the third person. Significantly, "Brekhunov" means "braggart."

9. H. Bergen's 1904 translation, which appears to derive from an alternative and probably earlier text, continues: "Sometimes it seemed as if they were going down hill, sometimes as if they were ascending. Sometimes it seemed as if they were standing still, and that the snow-covered fields were moving past them." See p. 88, where the same idea recurs.

10. *printificated in Pullson:* Osip Paulson (1825–1898) was a compiler of primary school manuals. Petrushka is quoting from his primer, with some errors in his Russian.

11. *five holdings:* land allocated to the peasants for their use, after the Edict of Emancipation in 1861. Practices differed from region to region, but it is possible that this family's size (with five adult males) entitled it to five holdings.

12. *younger brother:* In the Russian, Tolstoy contradicts himself here, saying that this son is the eldest, whereas earlier he had said the second son was in charge of the homestead. This seems the better of the two alternatives, since it would also be a cause of dissension if the younger brother was in charge of the household because the older brother was in Moscow.

13. *Children...on top of the oven:* In a normal Russian peasant dwelling the large brick Dutch oven was the best place to sleep, being very warm. A high wide bunk running along the wall under the ceiling was the other sleeping place in the single, communal room.

14. *poem from Paulson:* Petrushka is mangling the first four lines of a well-known poem by Pushkin.

15. *hame strap:* The hames are two curved pieces of iron or wood forming the collar of a dray horse, to which the traces are attached. They are locked together like a pair of pincers. In a storm like this, once undone it would be very difficult to buckle them together again.

16. *covered himself with the ticking:* Just as Nikita is far less warmly dressed than Vassili Andreyich, so now he takes care of himself last. Mukhorty is covered with sacking, but Nikita wraps himself in the coarsest cloth of all, the ticking made of woven birch bark.

17. *thirty sazhen...to each desyatina:* One sazhen was 2.13 meters. One desyatin was 2.7 acres. The Goriachkin forest was 56 desyatinas—about 160 acres—and worth about 12,500 rubles. Vassili Andreyich proposes to pay an advance of 3,000 rubles (of which 2,300 are "borrowed" from church funds in his care) and 8,000 in total. The total price is thus a little short of the money Ivan Ilyich was so glad to get on taking up his final job (5,000 rubles annual salary and 3,500 rubles in moving expenses). The real value of the woodland is equivalent to two and a half years' salary for Ivan Ilyich.

18. H. Bergen's translation continues: "If it were God's will that he should wake up alive in this world, that he should continue to do the work of a servant as in former days, always taking care of other people's horses, and carting other men's rye to the mill, that he should again from time to time take to drinking, and afterwards solemnly vow never to touch another drop, that he

should give all his earnings to his wife and her cooper as he used to do, and be kept long waiting for that same old pittance—well, God's will be done.

"But if God were to command him to awaken in another world, where everything would be new and joyous, as once, in his early boyhood, the caresses of his mother, the games with other children, the meadows, woods, the sleigh rides in winter were new and joyous to him in this world, and if he were to begin an entirely new life there, quite different from the life he had been living here—well, God's will be done. Nikita now became wholly unconscious."

19. *candles...put back in their chest:* another bit of cheating. Vassili Andreyich didn't leave the worshippers' candles burning after the service but took them back for resale, as new.

Reading Group Guide

1. "The Death of Ivan Ilyich" and "Master and Man" are both stories about dying well or badly. How does Tolstoy think death should be faced? What makes dying difficult?

2. Read Tolstoy's other stories about death, like "The Snowstorm," "Three Deaths," "Memoirs of a Madman," "How Much Land Does a Man Need?" and "What Men Live By." Do his attitudes to death change as he comes closer to his own death?

3. E. M. Forster believed that birth and death present the novelist with insuperable difficulties. "We only know of them by report. Our final experience, like our first, is conjectural. Certain people pretend to tell us what birth and death are like...but it is all from the outside." Is Tolstoy's presentation of the experience of death "all from the outside"? Is it convincing?

4. Other writers have tried to describe dying from the inside: Giuseppe di Lampedusa, for instance, in Chapter 7 of *The Leopard*; William Golding in *Pincher Martin* and the last chapter of *Darkness Visible*; Ian McEwan in Part 2 of *Atonement*. There are many poems by Emily Dickinson, like "I heard a fly buzz when I died" or "Because I could not stop for death," that describe the subjective experience of death. How well do these authors compare with Tolstoy? What are they trying to tell us about death? Can you think of any other writers who attempt the difficult task of describing death from inside?

5. John Keats said, "We hate poetry that has a palpable design on us, and if we do not agree, seems to put its hand in its breeches pocket." Tolstoy's stories could be called examples of affective literature—they want to persuade us into a particular attitude to both life and death. Do we hate him for his palpable design on us, or do we accede? If we do accede, why? How has he persuaded us?

6. Tolstoy believed that there was a radical difference between attitudes to death in the well-to-do bourgeoisie and the impoverished peasantry. What were they? Do you think his views would still hold good for the different social classes of today?

7. Tolstoy has a strong satirical bent. What are the objects of his satire, and why? We tend not to think of him as a humorous writer—is his satire ever funny?

8. Tolstoy was an entirely idiosyncratic, independent freethinker. Many respected institutions were derided by him—the Church, the Law, the medical profession, even the theater. Where do you find mockery of such bodies in these stories? Why did Tolstoy attack them?

9. Tolstoy's style is renowned for its direct, simple truthfulness. Is this reputation justified? Is there an art in his artlessness?

10. There is no writer, perhaps, who has understood people as well as Tolstoy. He seems to be intimate with everybody and everything—not only people but animals and even objects. Can you find striking examples of his insight in these stories? Can you compare him to any other writers with comparable psychological insight and universal sympathy—George Eliot, for instance, or James Joyce?

A NOTE ON THE TYPE

The principal text of this Modern Library edition
was set in a digitized version of Janson, a typeface that
dates from about 1690 and was cut by Nicholas Kis,
a Hungarian working in Amsterdam. The original matrices have
survived and are held by the Stempel foundry in Germany.
Hermann Zapf redesigned some of the weights and sizes for
Stempel, basing his revisions on the original design.

MODERN LIBRARY IS ONLINE AT
WWW.MODERNLIBRARY.COM

MODERN LIBRARY ONLINE IS YOUR GUIDE
TO CLASSIC LITERATURE ON THE WEB

THE MODERN LIBRARY E-NEWSLETTER

Our free e-mail newsletter is sent to subscribers, and features sample chapters, interviews with and essays by our authors, upcoming books, special promotions, announcements, and news.

To subscribe to the Modern Library e-newsletter, send a blank e-mail to: **sub_modernlibrary@info.randomhouse.com** or visit **www.modernlibrary.com**

THE MODERN LIBRARY WEBSITE

Check out the Modern Library website at
www.modernlibrary.com for:

- The Modern Library e-newsletter
- A list of our current and upcoming titles and series
- Reading Group Guides and exclusive author spotlights
- Special features with information on the classics and other paperback series
- Excerpts from new releases and other titles
- A list of our e-books and information on where to buy them
- The Modern Library Editorial Board's 100 Best Novels and 100 Best Nonfiction Books of the Twentieth Century written in the English language
- News and announcements

Questions? E-mail us at **modernlibrary@randomhouse.com**
For questions about examination or desk copies, please visit
the Random House Academic Resources site at
www.randomhouse.com/academic